Thirteen Years
of
Christmas

Maria Elizabeth McVoy

VANTAGE PRESS
New York

Illustrated by Tanya Stewart

FIRST EDITION

Copyright © 2010 by Maria Elizabeth McVoy

Published by Vantage Press, Inc.
419 Park Ave. South, New York, NY 10016

Manufactured in the United States of America
ISBN: 978-0-533-16215-4

Library of Congress Catalog Card No: 2009902157

0 9 8 7 6 5 4 3 2 1

For my family:
Daddy, Mumzie, Matthew, Emily and E.J.
I dedicate to you my first book.
Merry Christmas!

Contents

Preface

Christmas has always been a very special time of year for me. Among other notable attributes, Christmas is a time of great stories. The day itself celebrates the story of a child born in a stable in Bethlehem. From that humble beginning has come a multitude of stories—two hundred centuries of imagination and creativity—immortalizing the day a savior was born into an annual celebration of reclamation, love and magic. To this esteemed pantheon, I bring the fruits of thirteen years contemplating the spirit of Christmas.

As a young child, I was fascinated by the Christmas traditions in other countries. In America, we have Christmas trees from our German heritage and stockings hung by the chimney from our English brethren. But I was fascinated also by the traditions we had not adopted: the French put out shoes for their gifts and have twelve Christmas desserts; the English have a tradition of opening brightly wrapped tubes of paper, bound in twists at the end like peppermint candy, filled with a few small, delightful gifts. I never did quite get around to putting out shoes for Père Noël, but the Christmas I was fourteen I decided to make English crackers—a surprise for my family to open on Christmas morning. My passion as a child was writing stories and poems. When I decided to make crackers for my family, it seemed only natural to place a story inside. This spontaneous gift quickly became a tradition of writing one Christmas story every Christmas Eve—for what has now been thirteen years—and wrapping it up as crackers for my family to open at breakfast the following morning.

I usually write these stories on Christmas Eve, after the tree is lit and decorated. It is so much easier to write a Christmas story curled up in front of a glowing tree, with Christmas carols emanating from the nearby stereo system. I was a child when I first began to write on the subject of Christmas. My thoughts were perhaps simple, as children are wont to make any subject. But as I grew, so did my conception of this holy and miraculous holiday. Christmas became not just the time for finding the perfect gift for a friend or making a magical wish, but also a time for giving of oneself—not in monetary terms, but in time, forgiveness, and love. Too often we are so caught up in the bustle of our busy lives that the most precious things are lost—a moment of thanks, a kiss, a prayer. Christmas becomes all the more sacred as a time when we remember to give thanks, to show affection and to pray— not just for the things we desire, but for the people we cherish and for all the blessings bestowed upon us, however elusive.

I invite you into my childhood, to transgress time and space, into the imaginative mind of a fourteen-year-old girl. And from there I invite you to leap through time with me, Christmas by Christmas, as the day may become less simple but the spirit of the season remains constant. I have created what I hope is a testament to the magic, love and hope that Christmas should hold for all of us.

May the blessings of Christmas be upon you and all those you love, forever.

—Maria Elizabeth McVoy

Thirteen Years
of
Christmas

December 23, 1996
Age 14

The Most Beautiful Girl at the Christmas Dance

Her eyes were blue, silver-blue, the shimmering color of the ocean at midday. Her hair was the rich, dark brown of the mahogany chair on which she was seated. She was the most beautiful girl in the room, and yet she sat alone, with a sad smile on her face, as if she understood why it was that the most beautiful girl at the Christmas dance should sit alone and also as if it pained her to understand why.

She was not quite so very alone, though. Boys would come up to her, hands outstretched to ask her to dance; but she neither took their hands nor looked into their hopeful eyes. It took only a few moments of this before they understood, apologized embarrassed, and left her to once more sit alone.

It was always like this for Clara. She had schooled herself since she was a very young girl to pay it no mind and, as the years passed, she had convinced herself that she did not mind it; but it is only to a certain extent that a young girl can lie to herself like this, and each year it had gotten harder and harder to smile at all, especially at Christmas.

Since she was a little child, her mother had read her the story of the Nutcracker doll; and she had often wished, like that Clara, she might experience some magic

1

on Christmas Day that would spirit her away to a land of magic and sweets: a land where she could fit in. But Clara had no Godfather Drosselmeir to give her a magical doll. As each Christmas passed, the same as the one before, there was no magic either; and perhaps it was this painful disappointment that made Christmastime so much harder to bear than any other time in the preceding year.

This Christmas showed no signs of being any different from any other Christmas. She had already been visited by several would-be dancing partners; and when another approached, she turned her head toward his footsteps so that her dark curls framed her blue eyes and her sad smile. Perhaps she should have long ago ceased to hope that, someday, someone would come along who did not care that she would not meet his eyes and take his hand when he offered it. Perhaps she should not still turn her head with such childish hope, but she was still young enough to believe in magic and miracles, and it was Christmas—the season of hope.

"Good evening, and Merry Christmas to you," said a voice by her shoulder, as if its bearer had knelt down beside her chair to converse.

"And to you, also," she replied, hope rising in her voice and making its soft, silvery tone tinkle like faraway Christmas bells.

"If the next line on your dance card isn't taken, would you honor me with a waltz?"

She stiffened; this was the point in a conversation she knew too well. The moment she raised her hand to accept, they always knew. She had heard it so many times, from so many different gentlemen, that she could almost hear his forthcoming accusation and embarrassed apology. She braced herself as she raised her hand, telling herself that he would only be another disappointment

and that she didn't care. When, in her heart, she did care and she still held the dog-eared, faded remnants of hope close to her heart, like a letter read so many times that its contents are beyond recognition—the paper itself saved only as a token of some happy memory that will never be forgotten. She raised her hand and his fingers closed over hers. Her feet moved before she told them to, and she found that she was standing with his other hand on her waist—and her other hand was raising the trailing hem of her gown from the dance floor—and. . . .

She was dancing!

She had waited so many Christmases for that moment that she did not ever want it to end. The dance in which he had asked her to accompany him was a comfortably slow one that she had learned the steps to years before, without any hope of ever exercising them. As she danced the familiar steps, steps she had danced so often in her dreams, she wondered if this too was not just a dream and that she should not awaken any moment in the mahogany chair. Time passed and another dance began, but she did not awaken.

They danced four turns together and, as they danced, Jim (for that was the boy's name) quoted humorous lines from Shakespeare and Charles Dickens till she was laughing so hard she could barely get a breath between laughs. It had been many Christmases since she had laughed so much. It felt good to laugh and to dance and to guess from what Shakespearean play or Dickens novel he was quoting.

"Our host just unveiled a flaming pudding; shall we sample it?" he asked her after the fourth dance.

"Certainly!" she answered, suddenly famished from all the wonderful exercise.

"I'll just be a moment then."

4

Too late she realized what he had said and, as his footsteps faded toward the banquet tables, sheer terror fell over her. She groped around with her hands, searching for a chair or a table or a wreath of holly that would tell her where she stood. But her fingers came in contact with nothing; and she was alone, utterly alone. She collapsed on the floor, tears streaming down her cheeks, not caring if anyone saw, for in her terror she was past caring.

"Clara," his voice spoke behind her.

Jim! Oh, now he would know. She could hide it from him no longer.

"Are you feeling faint?"

She could feel him helping her to her feet, as if from a great distance. He guided her to a chair and sat beside her, trying to make her tell him what was wrong, trying to make her smile, trying to make her lift her head and look at him. She raised her head slowly, opening wide her blue eyes. He knew—she could tell by his voice—he knew that her wide silvery-blue eyes couldn't see him. He knew why the most beautiful girl at the Christmas dance should sit alone. He knew that she was blind; and with that knowledge he would leave her, as had all the other boys.

She could hear the rustle of silk beside her as he shook his handkerchief from his pocket, gently lifted her face, and dried her eyes. He held her hand tenderly as he raised her to her feet and led her out onto the dance floor. As they again began to dance, Clara could feel a different sort of tear sliding down her cheek.

December 24, 1997
Age 15

The Last Stroke of Midnight

She stared out at the snowflakes swirling over the frosty grass outside the living room window. It was night, but did not seem so because outside it was bright as day. The layers of purest white reflected the light of the moon as they would the light of the sun—the brightness of midday in the poem *'Twas the Night Before Christmas.* Had it been as cold inside that living room, as it was outside, the droplets on her eyelashes and cheeks would have been flakes of snow; but it was warm and cozy in that living room, and the droplets on her cheeks were only tears.

She turned her head away from the window, as if looking at something as lovely as the first snowfall hurt more than anything. Tears streamed unchecked down her cheeks. *I hate winter*, she thought passionately. *I hate it; it's so cold and unfeeling and . . . and . . .* But she didn't hate it, not really. It had been her favorite time of year, once, and Danny's (but no, she mustn't think about Danny, not now, not at Christmastime), but now winter was filled with too much sorrow. And as she remembered playing in snow forts, and having snowball fights, and building snowmen, the tears flowed afresh.

She got up from the chair and stumbled into the kitchen. Blinded by tears, she banged her hip against the edge of the counter, and fell in a heap, knowing full well she wouldn't be able to get up again without help.

Through bleary eyes she saw a doodle of Kilroy peeking over the edge of the counter, where Danny must have scribbled it just before he left two years previous. She felt terribly alone.

She was not alone in the kitchen; their white kitten Missy was nosing through some cookie crumbs someone had neglected to sweep away. Missy turned toward her when she fell, nonchalantly walked over, and climbed up into Karen's lap rubbing her soft, white head against Karen's shoulder as if to say, "Don't worry, it will be all right." or "It doesn't matter, I love you anyway!" Karen put her arms around Missy and held her tight. Missy squirmed and, after Karen released her, curled up in her lap to await morning.

While stroking the back of that tiny white cat, and trying to shift into a more comfortable position without disturbing her, Karen remembered something her mother had told her, so very long ago.

*   *   *

"Mommy, tell me again when it's the best time to make a wish. Tell me again, please."

Linda gathered little Karen into her arms, and her voice took on the soft singsong of a lullaby:

"Wishes are words of hope and happiness,
Dreams of a lover and a soft caress,
Words of wisdom and songs of joy,
Love for every girl and boy.

7

"A wish can be made at any time:
A soft-spoken word or a practiced rhyme.

"But there is one time of year—
When Christmas is near—
When, whether you're glad or blue,
Your wish will always come true.

"When the first snowfall is past
And this night is the last,
Till Christmas bells will ring
And little angels sing—

"When the last stroke of midnight ceases to sing,
And the first stroke of Christmas has not yet to ring—
Then gather the wishes dear to your heart
And the best of them all from the others part.
And yell it out for the whole world to hear,
Before the stroke sounds that says Christmas is here!

"Then will your wish surely come true
And the blessings of Christmas shower down upon you."

*   *   *

Karen looked up at the kitchen clock—it was nearly midnight. *Perhaps I will make a wish,* she thought, and waited in the semi-darkness for the clock to strike midnight.

And then, as if encouraged by thoughts of her mother, her mind turned to Danny. *Oh Danny,* she thought, *dear, sweet, darling Danny. When are you coming home to me, Danny? When will I see my sweet Danny boy again?* Then she remembered why it was she could

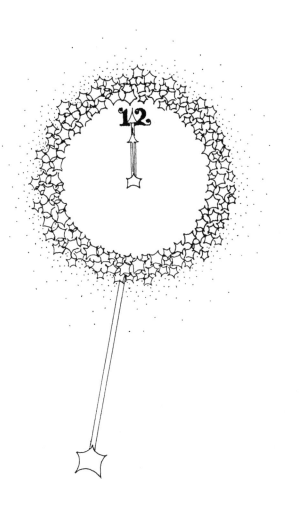

not rise without help. She remembered the skiing accident. She remembered falling down that steep mountain, and the sickening crunch as her leg hit the tree. *Oh Danny, come home to me. Even if you can no longer love me. Come home, I need you.*

The clock struck midnight: Dong . . . Dong . . . Dong . . . Dong . . .

"Oh Danny boy, I love you," she whispered.

Dong . . . Dong . . . Dong . . .

"Come home to me Danny boy," she whispered louder.

Dong . . . Dong . . . Dong . . . Dong . . .

"Danny boy . . ." she whispered, a final time, louder still.

Dong . . .

". . . come home to me."

A key turned in the lock, and the door swung open. And there standing in the doorway was Danny, still in his army medical corps uniform. She opened her mouth to call a greeting or to scream—she did not know, for she could not utter a word. In two quick steps he crossed through the foyer and stood over her, his boyish grin seeming all the more boyish from beneath his uniform cap. *Oh, why did he have to see me like this, helpless on the floor?* she thought.

He lifted her up in his strong arms, supporting her lame leg with one hand, and encircling her slender waist with the other. "My darling," he whispered, then kissed her again and again. And, as if he had heard her unspoken question, he said between kisses, "You're just as I remembered you for two long years . . . You're perfect."

She opened her mouth to deny this, but he stopped her protests with a kiss.

"You look like a dream. You're the most beautiful thing I've ever seen!"

She pressed her lips against his to stop those beautiful words, but they went on unspoken and healing to her once saddened soul.

And the sun rose on a Christmas morning that was as perfect as the sweetheart a soldier had once left behind.

December 24, 1998
Age 16

A Special Gift

He stood on the front porch of his house, on Christmas Eve, with his eyes closed feeling the lacy snowflakes land on his cheeks like icy kisses. Andy thought he heard a muffled sound behind him and then he fell tumbling into the powdery snow. He laughed and sat up as Eva brushed white specks of snow from her long, dark hair. They had been best friends for who knew how long and were as close as twins.

She smiled at him. "Sorry, I tripped . . ."

"You did no such thing," he laughed. "You pushed me on purpose."

"No, I—" A feather-soft snowball caught her last words. This began their re-enactment of World War I, as each dug a trench and hurled snowy bombs at the other.

Three hours and many snowballs later, they stumbled into the house, too cold to continue their mock battle. Andy's house was decorated for Christmas, with holly and evergreen branches on every mantle and over every door. There were tiny snow scenes on various shelves and bookcases, and in the corner of the living room was a magnificent tree hung with Christmas balls and glass figurines that sparkled as the many colored lights caught them in their warm glow.

Eva collapsed in a chair by the table and pulled the stuffed camel, Humphrey, into her arms, as Andy

whipped them up a couple of steaming cups of hot chocolate. "He's so solemn," Eva said. Andy opened his mouth to protest, but Eva continued, "No, I don't mean grumpy." He smiled at that, "I mean he looks wise and peaceful, as if he knows and understands . . ."

"Maybe he does!" Andy said smiling, again, before turning back to the cocoa.

A few minutes later, he watched her stroke Humphrey over his cup of hot chocolate. Her dark hair hung in snow-soaked strands around her face and over her shoulders, and her dark eyes were laughing at him, as if to say, *You look just as messy*. Even with her hair wet and tangled and her nose red from the cold, Eva was beautiful—and he hadn't gotten her a present.

It wasn't that he had forgotten. How could anyone forget to get someone a Christmas present if they had snowball fights or played tennis with them every day of the year? No, he hadn't forgotten her; he simply didn't know what to give her. No, that wasn't it either: he wanted it to be special. He could think of lots of things that Eva would love for Christmas; and in fact, as it is with all good friends, if it came from him he knew she would love it no matter the item. But still, he wanted it to be special.

"On the first day of Christmas my true love gave to me a partridge in a pear tree . . ." sang Eva. "Andy, who do you think would want a partridge in a pear tree for Christmas?"

"You would, you love pears."

"Yes, but the partridge . . ."

"What about the partridge?"

"Who would want a bird for Christmas?" she asked.

"Oh, I don't know, probably someone who has everything else, and wants something new," he countered, smiling.

She laughed; she had a beautiful laugh. "Seriously."

"Well, how am I supposed to know? How did we get on this subject anyway?"

"I was singing."

"Then let's sing . . ."

They wound their way through "Silent Night," "O Christmas Tree," "O Holy Night," "O Come All Ye Faithful," "Joy to the World," "Hark the Herald Angels Sing," and then started on "There's No Place Like Home for the Holidays," and "Chestnuts Roasting on an Open Fire."

"Wouldn't it be dangerous to roast chestnuts on an open fire?"

"Just sing, Eva!" And they began "The Christmas Waltz."

She looked at the clock on the mantelpiece as they started singing "I'll Be Home for Christmas."

"Andy," she said, as he sang ". . . We'll have snow and mistletoe . . ."

"Hmmmm?" he said before whistling the rest of the song.

"I should go, I have to be at Jenn's to carol at seven, but . . ."

"But?" he said smiling, as she whispered into Humphrey's plush ears—something she did often, as if Humphrey would be able to convince Andy when she failed.

"I'll come back and exchange presents with you before midnight. That is, if you won't change your mind."

He shook his head. He wasn't going caroling this year; he never went. "And break our wonderful traditional argument about my going?" He laughed.

She laughed too. "Not that I really thought you would."

Once she was gone, Andy collapsed on his bed and gathered Humphrey, his favorite stuffed animal, into his arms. The stuffed camel's glossy, gold coat was soft beneath his fingers, and warm because Eva had been holding him. He racked his brain for a good present for Eva. At least, that's what he started doing; he ended up just thinking of all the fun they had had in past Christmases. The scenes seemed to fly past him like the landscape seen through the windows of a fast-moving train.

The time he had taught Eva to ice skate and they held hands so she wouldn't fall.

The winter they had built an igloo and spent a whole afternoon playing Eskimos.

The night Eva had slept over on Christmas Eve, when they tried to stay up all night and see Santa Claus, but fell asleep around eleven and awoke to find Santa had come while they'd slept.

The year of the Christmas pageant at school, when Eva had played Mary and Andy the shepherd in charge of all the little kids who were playing sheep. One of the kids had broken her leg the week before the pageant and Andy had carried her on his shoulders, much to her delight!

The afternoon when they had made a huge gingerbread castle and ate the whole thing. (They didn't eat anything that Christmas, their stomachs hurt so much.)

The scenes came before him one after another, as he stroked Humphrey's golden coat, and slowly he fell asleep.

When he awoke, it was almost time for Mass. He bundled into his coat and headed out into the snowy streets. He walked along not thinking of anything, humming "The Twelve Days of Christmas"—*Andy, who do you think would want a partridge in a pear tree for Christmas?*—and enjoying the cool Christmas air. Finally he entered the doors of the church, sliding into a pew just as the Mass started. He sat there during Mass, smelling the burning candles and the scent of holly and incense. Afterwards he went up to the altar and looked down at the Crèche set. He loved this Crèche because it seemed so real. Mary looked tired but happy. Joseph looked proudly and tenderly at his foster son. Jesus had a look of pure love on his face. The shepherd and the three kings were in awe, and the little lambs and the camel had a look of peace and wisdom on their faces. Then he knew, he knew what to get her for Christmas. He knew what gift would be special!

Five minutes later, he once again stood on his front porch, but this time with his eyes open. He held the gift from Eva in his hands, a gilt ornament of a tiny partridge—the veins of gold in the bird's plumage glinted in the silver moonlight, like the gold star of David at Eva's throat. As he held the miniature bird in his hands and watched Eva walk home, he smiled to himself. Eva's long, dark hair mingled with Humphrey's golden fur as she hugged him close, protecting him from the flakes of snow that were slowly swirling out of the sky.

December 24, 1999
Age 17

Ice-Blue Tissue Paper

It was a round table, dark brown and well worn as many dinners and many projects had happened upon it. That evening it was covered with a white tablecloth—plain white, not the tablecloth with a pattern of interlocking silver angels embroidered on the hem. Everyone at the table noted its absence as they noted the absence of the crystal angel candlesticks, but no one mentioned their absence. Three people sat around the familiar round table: a man, a young woman, and a boy. They sat with smiles on their faces and warm words on their tongues, but with their eyes each noted the plain white tablecloth, the pewter candlesticks and the empty chair at which none would look. Finally each came to a point where they could pretend no longer and tears silently rolled down their cheeks, but they chose to ignore that as well.

In the next room there was a Christmas tree: a beautiful Douglas fir decorated with glowing ornaments in all the colors of the rainbow. They had put it up that afternoon just as they always had, for it was Christmas Eve. But the tree was not the same either; there were ornaments missing: a white dove on a blue silk ribbon, a pair of glass ballet slippers, a set of exquisitely painted ornaments that depicted the gifts given in "The Twelve Days of Christmas." All these were missing. They were missing because, like the tablecloth and the candlesticks, they

18

were locked in the mahogany chest in the attic—Elaina's chest.

David, for that was the man's name, wiped his eyes with the back of his hand and smiled sadly at his children. "She wouldn't have wanted us to grieve this way," he said softly, almost more to himself than his offspring.

The young woman laughed, a real laugh though it had tears in it. "She would have said, 'Laugh and be merry, for it is Christmas and I shall never be far away from you ever.' " Her voice trembled as she recited the litany that their mother had said to them every Christmas when she had been called away to the hospital on emergency.

But last summer it had been she who had been the emergency. It was she who had been hit headlong by a drunk driver and killed, though not instantly. Her death had been slow, several days of internal bleeding that wouldn't stop. David thought of that now—thought of her lying motionless on the hospital bed, unmarked, save for a shallow gash beside her left eye where a piece of flying glass had caught her face. She had looked so beautiful. He had sat beside her for hours and held her hand. For a moment he had thought her hand had tightened on his— then she slipped away. Dr. Elaina MacKenzie had given her life to working in the emergency wing of the hospital and had died a victim of such an emergency.

David stood up and held his arms out to his children. He embraced them both: Alex—*what kind of woman would name her daughter Alexandra?*—almost eighteen and ready for graduation from the dance academy that she had attended since she was four; and Ryan, a typical ten-year-old still on his baseball streak, living in the Phillies cap his mother had bought him last July for his birthday.

"It will never be the same without her," their father whispered. "But we're still together and don't think I love you any less than she did." At that they all cried, for though Elaina had been the Christmas elf—always the one to buy the best gifts and stash them away in her chest for Christmas—and though she had never missed one of Alex's ballet recitals or one of Ryan's baseball games, David had been ever-present in his children's lives. Many a Christmas or day after school the children had come home to their father, who would lay out toasty mugs of hot chocolate and ask them how their days had gone. He would tuck them in at ten and Elaina would kiss each forehead gently before going to sleep in the early morning hours. They had been a family, not perfect, but real and happy.

"You should sleep. You'll want to get up early and open your presents," David said into Alex's hair.

"What's the point?" Ryan sniffled. "There won't be any presents from Mom!" It was true. Elaina had always kept her special presents in her chest until Christmas. It was a big chest made of well-seasoned mahogany with a well-polished brass lock. The key was small, only an inch and a half at most, and Elaina had worn it around her neck always. They had bought the chest the summer they were married in Scotland and she made him promise never to open it—he hadn't. The presents she had kept inside were always wrapped in ice-blue tissue paper, with tiny cards written out in silver. No, there would be no presents from her this year in ice-blue tissue paper.

David only hugged them closer and then sent them off to bed.

*   *   *

Alex lay in the dark, remembering how her mother had taken her to the dance academy when she was four and enrolled her in ballet. She had taken her out afterwards and bought her pretty leotards, stockings and shoes. "If you always dress beautifully when you dance, you'll always dance beautifully," her mother had said. To that day Alex always danced in elegant outfits, never in the leg warmers or T-shirts and shorts that her friends sometimes wore. Her mother never missed one of her recitals or performances, until this winter when she had missed *The Nutcracker*. It was the biggest performance all year—a month of performances—and Alex had been cast as the Snow Queen. It was a difficult role—the second most difficult next to the Sugar Plum Fairy—and her mother had been so excited for her. Alex's eyes got heavy and she fell asleep, a tear staining her pillow.

It was opening night. Alexandra (she always used her full name in the dance programs) was standing backstage in her white and silver outfit. There was a faux diamond tiara which her mother was pinning into her hair. Elaina kissed her daughter's glitter-freckled cheek and, when she drew back, Alexandra could see silver glitter on her mother's lips. "Break a leg, sweetheart!" she said—as always conscious of stage superstition. "I'll be watching from the front row, so don't forget to smile." As her mother hurried off to get her seat in the house, Alexandra stationed herself behind one of the side curtains, waiting for her cue. . . .

Alex rolled over in her sleep and smiled as her dream continued.

*   *   *

Ryan lay in the darkness throwing and catching a baseball and staring at the ceiling. Mom had never missed one of his baseball games until this summer. The last game she hadn't been there; he had pitched the whole game—coach had never let him pitch more than an inning in the past. *Mom would have been so proud,* he thought. But she hadn't been there. Ryan shoved the baseball beneath his pillow and closed his eyes.

It was the last baseball game of the season. Coach took him aside before the game and told him, if he could handle it, he'd pitch the whole game! Ryan ran over to his mother and told her. She picked him up in her arms and swung him around in a circle. "Show them what you've got, kiddo!" she said, and sent him back to his team. "I'll be cheering you on the sidelines!" she called after him and sat down on the bleachers, leaning slightly forward to watch, sweat forming beads on her forehead. Ryan stepped up to the mound, relaxed, and started throwing a few practice pitches. . . .

Underneath his pillow, Ryan's hand found the baseball and held it; a smile twitched at the corners of his mouth as his dream commenced.

*   *   *

David lay in the king-sized bed feeling oddly small. This was his first Christmas without her. If he closed his eyes he could still smell the orchid-laced perfume she always wore. He could still see her glittering smile that always showed off her beautiful white teeth—*After four years of braces I have a right to show off my teeth,* she had said more than once. He felt tears pool in his eyes and he closed them. God, he missed her! He felt like they say amputees might feel, as if their missing appendage were just invisible and not gone.

Tomorrow would be difficult: Elaina had been so much a part of their Christmas tradition. Early Christmas morning, even earlier than Ryan, she would get up and go to the attic. Then she would go downstairs and set the table for Christmas breakfast with the embroidered white tablecloth, the crystal candlesticks and a white rose with a sprig of holly in a vase at the center of the table. She would place her, often lumpy, ice-blue tissue-paper-wrapped packages under the tree before she put on the old Christmas records that she had listened to as a child. Elaina wasn't much of a cook, but she would fry up sausages with a mixture of special spices (the recipe of which she refused to disclose) that she saved only for Christmas. Later, after they opened their presents, she would call them to breakfast by ringing a little bell.

No, Christmas just wouldn't be the same. He could crack open the chest and try to recreate Christmas morning without her, but he refused to break his promise never to open the chest. He pressed his hands to his face and felt the tears trickle between his fingers. He slept.

He was standing on the hill in Scotland where they had been married. Behind him, he knew, was the chapel and below was the wind-tossed heather of the highlands. He heard a noise behind him and Elaina's slender arms crept about his waist; he stiffened trying to keep his face straight. He could feel her breath on the back of his neck and dissolved into laughter. "You," she accused, "are the most ticklish male I have ever met." He whirled around and kissed her, burying his hands in her long, dark curls . . .

In his sleep, David's face relaxed and his tears ceased to flow.

*   *   *

Ryan woke up from his sleep first. He lay in bed, unmoving, remembering his mom's sweaty face and the feel of the ball in his hand. It wasn't so much like a dream as like a memory. It was the same game that he had played in late August—they had won—except that Mom had been there. He slowly became aware of the deep scent of spicy sausages and the slow, scratchy hum of Mom's Christmas records.

*   *   *

Alex was the second to awaken, she could still feel the ballet shoes on her feet and see the silver glitter on her mother's lips. She didn't feel as if she had just dreamed, but as if she had just remembered. She sat bolt upright as her mind registered the scratchy sound of her mother's records and the smell of Christmas sausages.

*   *   *

David was the last to awaken. He lay in bed and remembered how Elaina's hair had tangled about her shoulders in the brisk Scottish wind. They had talked of going back to Scotland for their anniversary in late August but, of course, that had never happened. Now he felt as if it had happened and he had just forgotten. His eyes flew open as the smell of sausages frying overwhelmed his senses, accompanied by the faint scent of purple orchids.

*   *   *

They met at the top of the stairs, still smiling slightly from their dreams and excited with a Christmas expectancy that none had thought would come that year. With all assembled, they ran down the stairs—for all the world like a small herd of elephants—and stopped abruptly when they saw the Christmas tree. It stood in the corner where they placed it every year; hanging on the leafy branches were the white dove with the blue silk ribbon and the glass ballet shoes. The figurines from the "Twelve Days of Christmas" were there too, winding around the upper branches. And there, beneath the tree, were three lumpy packages wrapped in ice-blue tissue paper. . . .

For a moment they could hardly move. David slowly walked up to the tree and removed the three packages, handing one each to Alex and Ryan and laying his own on his lap. His fingers trembled as he held the small package. "You first, Alex," he whispered hoarsely.

Alex carefully removed the tag with *Alexandra* written in her mother's silver script, then pulled off the wrapping paper slowly. It was a box—a big box from a Paris dressmaker. Inside was a dress, a mid-calf-length gown that shimmered from pale lavender to blue as she held it up. It had a sweetheart neckline, butterfly sleeves and a full skirt. The dress was for the New Year's Ball at the academy. She knew it. The ball was an annual gathering of all the dance students. *I would like to be a fly on the wall at that dance some year,* her mother always said. *There can't be any ball more spectacular than one where the guests are all professional dancers.* "Oh Mom," she whispered, standing up and holding the dress in front of her. A small box fell out of the folds of the dress; it was ice-blue velvet. Alex brushed her tears away with the

25

back of her hand as she opened it: inside were tiny white pearl earrings set in white gold, each with an ice-blue sapphire.

David's eyes widened as he saw them, for they were Elaina's. She had worn them at their wedding and a few occasions since. *They're only for very special occasions,* she had always said with a wink.

With the earrings was a note: *The dress doesn't really need a necklace, just wear a blue silk ribbon, and I think these earrings should do well.* Alex didn't even bother to brush away her tears now. She carefully took out the silver knots in her ears and replaced them with the pearl and sapphire earrings. Then she smiled tearfully, "What did you get, Ryan?"

Ryan needed no further urging; he ripped off the tissue paper and stopped, stunned, as he beheld a glove, a new leather glove in black. *You're crazy,* Mom had said when he had asked for a black leather glove. *You play baseball in the summer; won't your hand get more hot in a black glove than a brown one?* He slid the glove on his hand and a baseball rolled out—signed by Mike Schmidt. He sat speechless with the ball in his hand and then burst into tears. Alex put her arms around him and they cried together.

David recognized the ball as well—it had been a gift from Elaina's dad for her twenty-fifth birthday.

Unnoticed by his children, David opened his own package. It was a twisted chain with a pendant in a Celtic knot pattern. She had worn this before they were married, before they bought the chest. The tiny key to the chest had displaced this pendant from her throat; she had worn it always—as did she still. Tears pooled in his eyes as he clasped the chain about his neck and felt the heavy silver settle cool on his chest.

They then opened the other presents under the tree. There were sweaters and skirts for Alex, and a new sled for Ryan. There were dress shirts and ties for David, and boxes of old-fashioned ribbon candy for all three. There were toys and clothes, movies and music, and then as they came around to the back of the tree there was another present wrapped in ice-blue tissue paper. It was a squarish package addressed to all three of them: *For my three musketeers—Davey, Alex and Ryan. Merry Christmas!*

David took the package and removed the paper. It was a picture frame of holly and roses wrought in silver. The picture itself showed a woman with long, dark curls and eyes like pools of liquid blue ice. She was wearing a sweater the color of her eyes and behind her was a wood covered in snow. It must have been flurrying when the picture was taken, for there was snow caught in her curls. She was smiling so that they could see her perfect white teeth . . . beside her left eye was a scar.

They said nothing as David placed the picture on the mantelpiece.

From within the kitchen, the tinkle of a bell sounded and they ran from the room, by instinct, to answer its call to breakfast. There was no one in the kitchen, but the table was set for Christmas with a snow-white tablecloth embroidered on the hem with a pattern of interlocking silver angels. There were red candles in crystal angel candlesticks and a platter of spicy sausages. In the center of the table was a vase with a sprig of holly and a white rose.

December 24, 2000
Age 18

Christmas in July

I'll never forget that last Christmas before my brother went off to college. There's something about Christmas which is very much about love and family and being a child again, whatever one's age. And that last Christmas seemed like the last little breath of childhood before Jamie went away to college and grew up. Not that Jamie would ever, really, grow up; Jamie would be "twelve-teen"—an age that you won't find in the common dictionary, which my father invented on the eve of my brother's twelfth birthday—forever. But even always being "twelve-teen," he would change in college and would never quite be the same big brother that he was before. And, I guess, that's why that last Christmas was so special.

It was summer—had I mentioned that?—and the earth smelled of summer blossoms: the citrus tang of wood sorrel, the tiny clover-like plant with little yellow flowers that tastes like homemade lemonade; the heavier overlaying scent of roses in sunshine yellow, deepest red, and a shade of the sunset that one would never find in a florist's shop; and the delicate frangrance of the little wild violets with the heart-shaped leaves. Jamie, Mom and Dad fought an ongoing battle against those violets every summer—a battle that the violets continued to win, much to my delight and their chagrin. It was midsummer, early

July to be precise, and that meant I was sleeping late in the mornings (or as late as Mom would allow—which, granted, wasn't that late at all), and lounging outdoors in the afternoons on an old striped bedspread—which we kids had always used as a picnic blanket—reading adventure novels and fairy tales.

That particular afternoon, the afternoon of the last Christmas, Jamie, Mom and Dad were working on the side yard—picking weeds and laying out mulch, digging and planting, pruning and shaping, and, as the case was, cutting down some little spruce trees.

Or, rather, they would have been cutting down spruces if the head gardener, namely Jamie himself, hadn't been putting up a terrific fight for the trees: "Mom, you can't cut down these trees. They're the only trees left in the yard . . ."

This was not quite true. There were indeed considerably fewer trees on our property than had been in past years. However, there was still the big Japanese maple soaking up sunlight outside the back window, and the two big holly trees which hugged the corner of the house in such a manner as to create a space for a child to play. I can remember spending many hours in that holly cave as a child, playing international spies and soldiers with Jamie. The street in front of our house was still lined with giant oaks, complete with little scampering squirrels. My favorite climbing tree still stood, not more than thirty feet away from the related discussion, even if its more useful climbing branches had been amputated. But I could see his point: enough trees had been cut down.

". . . Mom you can't, you just can't." And then a change came in his argument. I was in the house at the time, but even now I can see his silver-blue eyes—like the ocean at midday when the sun hits the water and turns it almost silver—light up like candles as his brain fell upon a solution: "All right, you may cut it down, but on *one* condition!"

"What condition?" replied Mom, who was used to Jamie's conditions and not sure if she was going to like or comply with this one.

"You may cut it down . . . only if we may make it into a Christmas tree." His voice had that light smiling tone to it and his blue eyes sparkled with that "twelve-teen" shine—the same shine that overtook his eyes the day after Christmas, when he began his countdown to the next one.

"Fine!"

That was how our last Christmas began, with an argument over cutting down a four-foot spruce tree that resulted in a four-foot Christmas tree in our living room. Five minutes after our July Christmas had been so declared, Jamie stumbled into the house—one can never seem to remember to step *up* into the house when one is carrying something—with our little Christmas tree clutched lovingly in his arms.

Jamie is a generally happy person; he smiles and laughs a lot, and is always making jokes, especially when the rest of us get on one another's nerves. When he's around, one can almost *see* the mood relax. It's just his nature. But at Christmastime he's so much happier, there's almost no comparison. I think the Christmas happiness that filled his face that July *made* it Christmas even more than did the tree.

Our little sister, Ellie, scampered downstairs to get the tree stand, her dark curls bouncing against her tan shoulders. For all that we were putting up a Christmas tree, we were dressed for summer in T-shirts and tank tops in place of our usual winter sweats and sweaters. Instead of the smell of Christmas cookies, the scent of lemon wafted out of the kitchen, betraying the fact that Ellie had been baking lemon-pecan wafers, a purely summer cookie.

A moment later, Ellie arrived with the tree stand as the opening notes of "White Christmas" tinkled out of the speakers to fill the house with Christmas cheer. Jamie stood in the center of the room, waiting with the tree in his arms and a look of pure happiness on his face. Between the three of us, we managed to set the little tree in the stand (with the help of a few rocks in the bottom, because the tree was too little to reach all the way down). And when we were finished, we had a little Christmas tree in our living room whose top branches reached only to Jamie's shoulder. It was tiny compared to our usual eight- and nine-foot trees, but that July it was perfect.

Ellie and I ran upstairs—with Mom's usual call of "Don't run!" following us—and crawled into the attic to search for decorations. We eventually brought down the big, green box with the stuffed ornaments. The stuffed ornaments were fabric with a print of a nutcracker or a star or a Santa, etc. . . . on one side and a soft piece of red or green fabric on the other, sewn together and stuffed with cotton. Jamie put the first ornament on the tree: a little patchwork star. We all followed suit and soon the little tree was covered in puffy, colorful ornaments. We then threaded some strands of tinsel into the branches to make the tree sparkle.

When we were finished, we stepped back and smiled at the little bit of Christmas that we had just created. A buzzer sounded from the kitchen, and Ellie answered its call. Minutes later, she emerged with a plate of lemon-pecan wafers, of which everyone partook.

As I surreptitiously bit into my fourth cookie, I noticed that Jamie was absent. Puzzled, I glanced around for him. Usually he would be curled up in the striped chair with some of his animals gazing at the tree. But he wasn't there. I got a cold feeling in the pit of my stomach; was he perhaps too old to curl up as usual and stare at the tree? Had he grown up over the summer and I hadn't even noticed? Had he simply meant to decorate the tree and then go on about his day as if nothing had happened? Had I been mistaken about that Christmasy look that I thought I'd seen in his eyes? I could feel tears pricking behind my eyes; I'd never wanted him to grow up and have no time for childlike games and joys.

The screen door creaked as it opened behind my back. I was still staring at the little tree, wishing my big brother would never grow up. Then I could feel his presence behind me and smell his deeply scented deodorant, which Ellie loves.

"Rose . . ." he said softly, an undertone to "Silent Night," which was playing on the entertainment system. I turned and he handed me a single rose, the deep pink of the summer sunset. I couldn't think of anything to say. "Merry Christmas!" he said with a smile and a flash of silver-blue eyes. He then handed a deep red rose to Mom and a pale yellow to Ellie, wishing them the same greeting. I raised the rose to my face and breathed in the deep summer scent, as Jamie turned off the CD player, sat down at the piano and began to play "Have Yourself a Merry Little Christmas." We all four gathered 'round and raised our voices.

"Have yourself a merry little Christmas, let your heart be light. . . ."

In that moment—as I stood there singing, with the rose in my hand, watching the summer sun light up the tinsel on the tiny Christmas tree—I knew that I would

never forget that last summer before my brother went off to college. I knew that, though he might change, in many ways he would always be "twelve-teen," and always be the big brother that I had played with in my holly tree. I knew, without a doubt, that I would never forget that Christmas in July.

December 25, 2001
Age 19

What Child Is This?

The phone rang! Josh groaned loudly and reached blindly for the receiver, fumbling for his glasses at the same time. "You must be joking!" he exclaimed, as his sleep-fuzzy brain finally registered what the voice on the other end of the phone was trying to convey. "But it's Christmas Eve . . ." he began, but the line was dead. Josh muttered a plethora of colorful metaphors as he climbed out of bed and headed for the shower. It was Christmas Eve and he had to work. He would have quit, were it not for the fact that it had taken him three weeks to find this job, and he badly needed the income to help pay for college—scholarships only went so far.

The shower water was cold, even when Josh turned the faucet all the way up, and he was running out of original phrases to describe his dissatisfaction with the way his day was turning out.

An hour later, clean and in no better a mood, Josh walked into work and stepped behind his cash register, with the required smile firmly in place. He glanced at the clock: 12:00 P.M. It was going to be a long day and a long night.

Outside it had grown dark. It was past dinnertime, and long since Josh had remembered that he hadn't eaten anything. And it was Christmas Eve. Christmas Eve! How could his boss do this to him? Christmas Eve was a day for wrapping last minute gifts and spending time with those you love, not slaving away for college tuition.

The glass door opened and a young woman walked into the store. She had long, red hair and big, brown eyes; she was smiling and her cheeks were flushed from the cold. A young man entered behind her; he was built like a football player or a marine, and on his shoulders was perched a little boy who couldn't have been over three feet tall. The young man lowered the boy to the ground. The latter then proceeded to dash about the store in wonder, as if this simple corner store had become a land filled with adventures. The young woman followed the boy laughing and calling for him to slow down.

Minutes later, the little boy emerged from behind a display case with a package of eight mini boxes of cereal clutched in his arms. His face was alight with pleasure and his eyes danced with joy at the treasure he had discovered.

Josh came out from behind his register and went up to the young woman. Her hand was resting lightly on the boy's shoulder, but Josh had no doubt that those slender fingers would tighten if the boy suddenly got it into his head to rush off. "I can help you over here."

She smiled. "Come on, munchkin, this way." She guided the boy over to Josh's register. She then lifted the boy up so he could place the package of cereal on the counter. The boy stood with his nose just barely over the top of the counter as Josh rang up the cereal. After the young woman had paid, he handed the cereal back to the boy, who smiled as if he had been given a present. All of Josh's pent-up annoyance and anger at his rotten day seemed to melt in the warmth of that smile. He could feel the corners of his mouth twitching in response.

Spontaneously, he spoke as the young woman ar-

ranged the change in her wallet. "I had the most awful day, today." She glanced up with sympathy. "But seeing him," he nodded at the little munchkin, who was chattering to the young man about his cereal, "I guess it wasn't such a bad day after all." He searched her eyes for understanding and found it.

She reached down and picked up the boy, balancing him on her hip. "Say good-bye, munchkin."

The boy turned a pair of wise, blue eyes toward Josh and smiled once again. "Bye-bye!"

Then they were gone, out the door and into the night. But the happiness that they had brought to Josh's Christmas Eve remained. He smiled, and this time it was real.

December 25, 2001
Age 19

Pandora's Box
or
The Last Paper Crane

Cecily folded the Friday paper and laid it on the bench beside her. She could not really think of a good reason why she had picked it up in the first place, as it was Monday night, and she had already read that particular paper at least once a visit in the past five visits to the hospital. She wasn't even normally one to pick up a newspaper and read it on a regular basis; her friends tended to be her own personal media, giving her the most recent snatches of news, along with some fascinating editorial bits that the papers would never include. No, she couldn't think of a reason, beyond the fact that reading a three-day-old newspaper kept her mind occupied just enough to keep her from bursting into tears. And she had cried so many times in the past months that any break from the outpour was a welcome relief, even if it was for reading old news.

It was late, well past ten at night, and technically she shouldn't have been at the hospital at all; it was well past visiting hours and hospitals were not generally known for bending visiting rules. However, in the past few months, Cecily had become fairly familiar with the hospital staff and one of the nurses had promised that she could visit after Michael's operation. They had originally planned to perform the operation the week after Christmas, but Michael's condition had worsened. Cecily had been called four hours previous on her cell phone by one of the nurses, informing her that Michael had just been sent into surgery. She had run four red lights to get to the hospital, only to be informed that under no circumstances would she be allowed in the room during the operation. Betsy, the nurse on duty at the service desk, took pity on the distraught young woman and had promised to allow her up to see Michael after the surgery.

She closed her eyes against the tears and lay her head back against the wall behind her chair. Her hands clutched a box in her lap, as if it were Pandora's box after it had been opened to wreak pestilence over mankind—the box that, then, contained hope. The box was not wrapped; it was a small, cedar chest, which she had received when she graduated from high school. The lock had never worked, but it was a beautiful chest nonetheless. It had carried many things since she had received it: letters from friends in Europe, photographs of her family, little trinkets that she picked up in random shops that carried such items. But tonight it held something much more dear to her—tonight, it too held hope.

As she sat on that stiff hospital sofa, her mind traveled back over the past several months. She recalled the night, it seemed a hundred years ago now, when Michael told her that his cancer—which they had thought he was cured of in high school, before he and Cecily had even met—had apparently not been cured and that he was dying. The doctors had given him six months, a year at best; even with chemotherapy, radiation and surgery, he had only months to live. Cecily had cried and screamed. She'd cursed every deity and higher power she could name— being a theology major, that was quite a few. Michael had

41

just sat there and watched her, tears flowing freely down his face. Finally she had run out of breath and snuggled up beside him with her head over his heart, listening to the steady beat that reminded her he was still alive, for now.

They ignored it for as long as possible: ice-skating, playing endless games of chess (at which they were about on par), attending concerts and the theater, dancing, watching old black and white films, and taking long walks at night under the stars. But it was barely five weeks later that Michael had to be checked into the hospital. In almost no time, Michael's always slender figure wasted away to skin and bone. His fair complexion became as yellowed as the old parchment manuscripts which Cecily was using as the main source for her senior thesis.

His body may have been dying, but his mind was sharp as ever; Michael bombarded her with pop quizzes on obscure film quotes before she even made it through his door. He thought up riddles that would have given the Sphinx herself a headache. She bought a magnetic travel chess set and they had tournaments on a stolen food tray, which they hid in his closet before she left each day.

But the project, which would eventually take up much of their time together and apart, was conceived by Cecily just a month after Michael was checked into the hospital. Cecily had been in the library, supposedly looking up material for her thesis, which was due in a matter of months. But she had somehow taken a wrong turn and ended up in a stack dedicated to eastern mythology. It was as she sat curled up on the floor, reading a book of Japanese legends, that the idea came to her. There was a legend: to he who made a thousand paper cranes, the gods would grant a wish. Cecily immediately tucked the book of mythology under one arm and sought out a librarian, from whom she procured the location of an origami book. She recalled vaguely making cranes out of paper as a child, but could not recall exactly how it was accomplished.

Michael was thrilled with the project and went about learning to fold the delicate birds with great enthusiasm. Cecily wondered if she believed the legend of the thousand paper cranes. She wondered if Michael believed it. Or did they both fold cranes until they could almost fold them in their sleep, simply to keep their minds and fingers busy? Michael could very well believe in the legend. He believed in her poltergeist—a fact that never ceased to amaze her.

Cecily had discovered she had a poltergeist living with her freshman year. She had seemed plagued by practical jokes: her stereo would turn on at random hours of the day and night, CDs in her stereo would change, and the play lists on her computer would rearrange themselves. At first she had put the incidents down to happenstance, but slowly her mind had come to the realization that an intelligence was behind the chaos. It was a couple months into her first semester, when she realized that she was sharing her room with a poltergeist. It took her a while to become used to the idea of an invisible spirit rearranging her stuff every time she turned her back, and sometimes before she turned her back.

Michael, on the other hand, had taken Kirah, the poltergeist, in stride: saying hello to her promptly whenever he signed online or entered Cecily's room, and asking after her when he and Cecily spoke. Kirah, in turn, adored Michael. The computer always ran smoothly whenever Michael was online; his favorite music would start blaring from the speakers. Kirah would even touch up Cecily's

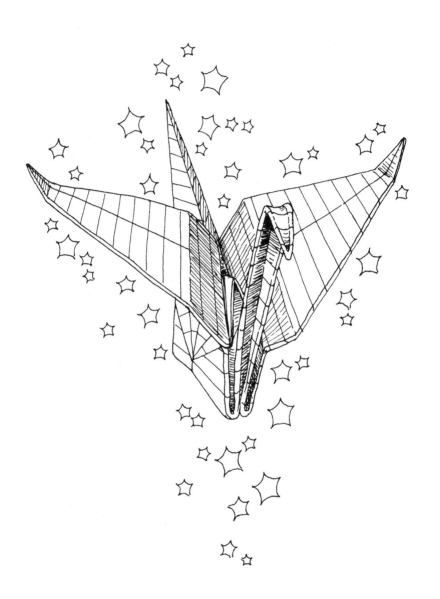

e-mails or instant messages with some imaginative colors or fonts.

Cecily had noted Kirah's presence in her room less and less; she was pretty certain that Kirah was spending a lot of time in Michael's hospital room. She only hoped that the mischievous poltergeist had the sense not to play with any of the machines regulating medicine in Michael's body. Cecily didn't think Kirah would ever hurt Michael on purpose, but she loved anything electrical— and might not understand that some machines shouldn't be tampered with by poltergeists. She would have warned the hospital staff; but what doctor or nurse would believe that a poltergeist might accidentally overdose one of their patients, simply because she couldn't stay away from electronics? As it was, Cecily had sternly told the air everywhere she thought the poltergeist might be, that Kirah should not tamper with any of the machines to which Michael was hooked up. Perhaps Kirah heard her, because none of them ever were touched by invisible hands.

"Miss Morgans, Miss Morgans?" a musical English voice called, scattering Cecily's thoughts, like the leaves left over from autumn caught in the cool winter wind. The voice belonged to Betsy, the nurse on duty who had promised to allow her access to Michael after the surgery was completed.

"Yes?" Cecily said, turning around with the cedar chest in her right hand, rubbing the beginning of a headache in her temples with her left.

"He's out of surgery and asleep in his room."

"How . . ." she began to ask.

"We won't know until morning. It . . ." Betsy paused, unwilling to say the words and yet knowing they would have to be said. "It doesn't look good, dear."

Cecily nodded, expecting this answer—yet, it still felt like someone wearing steel-tipped boots had just kicked her in the gut.

"I'm so sorry."

Betsy's condolence was inadequate, but it was heartfelt. Cecily managed a shaky smile in return. Ignoring the elevator, she headed for the stairs—needing the time it would take to climb five floors to compose her thoughts and emotions.

It was not very long, though, before she found herself in the doorway of Michael's room. It was a room meant for two, but Michael's skills in speech and diplomacy had paid off and kept him from having to share a room. The ledge by the window was filled with vases of flowers and potted plants; Cecily busied herself for a few moments, filling a pitcher from the sink in the bathroom and watering. There was a chair by the bed covered in an afghan, Cecily's chair. The book she had been reading him yesterday was still on the bedside table, *The Fellowship of the Ring* by J. R. R. Tolkein. Michael had been beside himself when he realized he wouldn't be able to attend the premier of the newest film based upon that book. The closet was almost empty; the clothes he had worn when he admitted himself to the hospital were there, and so were the magnetic chess set and stolen bed tray. Everything in that closet had been neglected for some time; it had been weeks since Michael had found the energy to play a game of chess. He hadn't even had the energy to fold paper cranes the past few weeks. It had been Cecily who folded cranes until her fingers ached with the effort.

The cranes they had folded were hung on the ceiling, nine hundred ninety-nine cranes. Cecily had been so excited when she first came up with the idea of folding cranes, that she had completely forgotten about the necessity of paper. Subsequently, their first crane ended up being folded out of a paper towel swiped from the bathroom. That crane hung over Michael's pillow. Some of the cranes were folded out of origami paper donated by Michael and Cecily's friends. But they had soon exhausted their supply of expensive paper and turned to anything they could find. Dozens of the birds were folded out of paper towels, napkins, wrapping paper from get-well gifts and, eventually, Christmas gifts. Cecily took to bringing discarded drafts of her thesis to Michael's room, where each sheet was carefully folded into a crane. The cranes varied in size and beauty. The earlier cranes, made by inexperienced fingers, were a little sloppy because of it.

Cecily's eyes panned over the ceiling, recalling a memory with each individual crane. When her eyes came to the very first crane, they dropped from the folded paper towel to the face on the bed, framed with dark curls. Michael was one of the few who did not lose his hair with the chemotherapy treatment. But even with his hair, he looked far from well. His skin was yellow and stretched tight over his bones. His face was etched with pain lines and those brown-black curls were touched with gray. He seemed so thin, so fragile, as if he would break if a single of those many cranes fell from the ceiling onto him. She stepped to the side of his bed, watching his chest rise and fall with ragged breaths through the thin, white sheet. A single tear slid off her cheek and made a stain on the fabric, as she leaned over and kissed his cold forehead.

She placed the box on his night table and opened the lid. Nestled inside the chest was a single paper crane. It was folded out of a sheet of notebook paper, which she had borrowed from someone in her dorm that night—she couldn't even remember the girl's name. The crane was folded perfectly, with the exact lines that came only after one had folded them before over a hundred times. It was the thousandth crane, the last paper crane.

Another tear fell onto the white sheet. Michael stirred in his drugged sleep—his breathing becoming even more difficult, by the sound.

She lifted the crane out of its box and held it against her heart for a moment, wishing with every fiber of her being that Michael would get well.

The radio behind her turned on and the last verse of Sarah McLaughlan's "Angel" filled the room: ". . . in the arms of the angel, may you find some comfort here. . . ." It was Kirah's way of comforting, Cecily knew, and she whispered her thanks to the invisible poltergeist.

As the radio turned itself back off, the silence was once again filled with Michael's ragged breathing. Cecily placed the last paper crane on Michael's chest, over his heart, and sat down on the chair holding his right hand in both of hers.

As Cecily's eyes once more filled with tears, the last paper crane blurred and seemed to grow and change. It was a live crane, white as snow and magnificent. The beautiful bird stood for a moment, contemplating Michael's pain-etched face. It reclined on his chest, with its wings folded and its head over his heart. Its compassionate, black eyes filled with tears.

Cecily blinked the tears away from her eyes. There was no live crane crying on Michael's chest—only a small paper crane remained, lying folded against his heart.

Michael stirred and his eyes opened, clear and bright with love. His right hand gripped her fingers with strength that he hadn't had in several weeks. In wonder, Cecily realized his breathing was normal and his hand was warm. His left hand reached up and gently touched her cheek, where the tears were drying. He sat up and

48

kissed her, cradling her face in his hand. His movement caused the paper crane to fall off his chest and onto the floor. Cecily reached beside her chair and picked up the fallen bird.

He raised a single dark eyebrow. "The last paper crane?"

She nodded, afraid if she spoke she would cry again.

He took the little paper bird in his hand and regarded it with wonder. "Thank you!" he whispered.

She wasn't certain if he was thanking her for making the crane, or thanking the crane for healing him—she didn't suppose it really mattered.

The radio turned on, blasting Christmas music, which would end when the nearest nurse discovered the source of the sudden noise in the hospital early Christmas morning. *Christmas morning*, Cecily thought in a daze, she hadn't even remembered that it was Christmas Eve. Every light in the room blinked on and off, changing color from red to green to bright blue with the beat of the music. Cecily and Michael smiled, acknowledging Kirah's celebration of Michael's recovery.

Cecily turned her eyes away from the colored light falling across the cranes on the ceiling, when she felt the gentle pressure of Michael's fingers on her chin.

"Merry Christmas!" he whispered.

As they kissed, invisible hands lifted the last paper crane, placed it in the little cedar chest and closed the lid.

For Mumzie—You always love my stories, so this one is just for you. Merry Christmas!

There's No Place Like Home

*And I do come home at Christmas. We all do, or we all
should. We all come home, or ought to come home, for a
short holiday—the longer the better . . .*
—Charles Dickens

He felt so alone. It was Christmas Eve—he fumbled for
his glasses, which had fallen to the floor under the bed,
and looked at the blue light of the little travel alarm
clock—Day actually, by a few minutes only. His clock
must have been fast; he could hear the deep resounding
peal coming from the bell tower of Notre Dame Cathedral.
Christmas Day. Somehow the expectancy that was supposed to come with that holiday had been lost somewhere—somewhere between the long flight to France and
the realization that any French he might have learned in
that one college course had long since wandered off.

Not that he wasn't pleased to be in France. He had
been thrilled when Elaine's parents had asked him to accompany them, and their daughter, to Paris for Christmas; it was a sort of honeymoon and Christmas gift all
entangled. And entangled was the way he felt. He was so
happy to be in Paris, to climb the Eiffel Tower, to walk the
long galleries of art in the Louvre. But it was Christmas,
and he missed his family. Elaine was his family now, but

it wasn't the same—not yet. They didn't have any traditions, not for Christmas.

He lay back and turned his head to regard his wife. Her slender figure was stretched out so that her toes touched the bottom edge of the bed. She lay on her stomach, her head facing away from her husband, breathing softly. Her long, silky hair was tangled behind her shoulders. She looked so beautiful, like a slumbering angel (a slumbering angel who sometimes sucked her thumb in her sleep, though she was not doing so now). She shivered in her sleep and he tucked the covers more warmly around her. He kissed her bare shoulder lightly, so as not to wake her, before covering it. What did his parents really think of Elaine, of the woman with whom he had decided to spend the rest of his life? He really wasn't certain. He thought they liked her; they'd asked her to family events before he'd announced their engagement. But he wondered sometimes if they had asked her because her presence made *them* happy, or because they knew it made *him* happy.

He rolled over roughly, wishing he could fall back asleep and stop thinking. But the more he tried to shut his eyes and relax, the more awake and restless he found himself. He remembered lying in bed on Christmas Eve as a child with a similar restless feeling—waiting for some obscene, but permitted, early hour to run downstairs and empty his stocking. His mother made stockings for all members of the family out of a fabric with a green holly pattern, and embroidered each person's name in red silk thread. He never quite figured out where she hid them from one Christmas to the next, but on Christmas Eve they were always hung carefully on the fireplace mantle, awaiting Santa.

Over the years the stockings had held various things.

They always included a tangerine wrapped in gold foil, and five little Russell Stover chocolate santas. Once, he and his sister, Jenny, had both received tiny Thundercats action figures, each only an inch tall. Another Christmas, he recalled, Jenny's stocking had contained a piccolo and his a set of drumsticks (the drums had been in the living room, out of sight). Sometimes the stockings contained delicate ornaments of carved wood or blown glass. Other times the stockings contained books, cassettes or videotapes. Every year a surprise awaited. Sometimes he could guess the gifts under the tree, but the stocking was always a mystery. And he had always loved mysteries.

The bells in Notre Dame were sounding the quarter hour (past which hour he didn't want to know). He climbed out of bed, making sure that Elaine was still covered and warm, and made his way into the adjoining room, where they had put up a little fir tree about three feet tall. His parents had sent a cardboard box to the apartment Elaine's parents had rented for them in Paris; he didn't want to know the price of the shipping. He stared at the cardboard box, not wanting to open it without Elaine, and yet wanting to run back to the bed and shake her awake, as he used to shake Jenny awake on Christmas morning when they were children.

Maybe he should just go take a walk, shrug off all his restlessness through physical exertion. What reason had he to be restless? After all, he was home—wasn't he? Elaine was his wife, the woman with whom he had chosen to spend the rest of his life. She was his family now, his home. And he loved her so much that sometimes it hurt. But so much of him wanted to be a little boy of five again, curled up on his mother's lap, listening to her recite *The Night Before Christmas.*

Behind him, he heard a gentle sigh and the soft plodding of bare feet on floorboards. Then Elaine's arms were around his neck and her soft hair was tumbling over his shoulders. She understood; he could tell without her saying anything.

Her left hand was clenched. It opened at his touch to reveal a small knife, such as newsboys had once used to cut the twine on bundles of newspapers. He took the knife and slit open the layers of tape on the cardboard box; he had wondered at times how much his mother added to the shipping price by using so much tape.

There was only one box inside, packed carefully as if it contained something breakable. The box was not labeled, but after some searching he managed to locate a card tucked away under the box. It read: *Alex, The rest of our gifts for you and Elaine are here; we couldn't afford to ship them all overseas. But we wanted to give you a touch of home for Christmas. Merry Christmas, darling. Love, Mother and Dad.* Alex tore open the red and gold paper and pulled off the lid of the department store box. Inside were two stockings with green holly patterns on them— embroidered in red silk thread on one was *Alex* and on the other was *Elaine.* Silently he passed his wife her stocking, the stocking that his mother made for every member of the family. He didn't trust himself to speak.

Inside Alex's stocking were five little Russell Stover chocolate santas, and a tangerine wrapped in gold foil. There was a tiny bottle of sixteen-year-old Lagavulin— one of his favorites. A little red book was nestled inside also, an ornament which contained in its pages the entire *The Night Before Christmas* poem. And last of all, there was a burned CD of his favorite Christmas songs.

Elaine's stocking also contained the chocolate santas and the tangerine. His parents had given his wife a little bottle of Chambord, which delighted her. At Thanks-

giving they had served cordials of Chambord for dessert; Elaine had commented that the spherical, gold-crowned bottle, filled with reddish-blue liqueur, resembled a Christmas tree ornament. Elaine's ornament was a blue book, and on its pages was Shakespeare's *Sonnet CXVI*. He recalled now, vaguely, Elaine and his father discussing poetry, over cocktails, at Thanksgiving. His parents had also included an Arthur Rubinstein (one of Elaine's favorite pianists) classical CD.

They turned and kissed, as if the gifts had been from one another. As they drew back, Alex thought he saw tears in Elaine's eyes.

Outside their apartment, morning had broken and people were filling the streets, on their way to Christmas Mass, singing Christmas songs at the top of their lungs: *"Vive le vent, vive le vent, vive le vent hiver."*

Alex took Elaine's hand and dragged her to the window. The words were unfamiliar—and he was pretty certain that the meaning of the words was different—but the tune was as familiar as turkey and cranberry sauce. Alex raised his voice, with the people of Paris, to greet Christmas morning: "Jingle bells, jingle bells, jingle all the way!"

As the carolers' voices faded into the distance, Alex kissed Elaine again. He held her close. Light from the rising dawn of Christmas over Paris illuminated them, and it felt like home.

December 25, 2003
Age 21

For Mumzie with Honey

She tossed and turned on the bed, overheated and aching, trying to get comfortable so she could just fall into sleep and escape for a little while. What hour it was she had no idea, but some sense told her that it was Christmas Eve. Her motherly instincts shrank at the realization, for she was not nearly prepared.

Since being struck ill the week before, she had been unable to so much as go down the stairs without exhausting herself. It had become an impossibility that she would be able to prepare for Christmas, as was her custom. But, she wondered as she lay uncomfortably, who would prepare if she were unable?

A soft, high voice jingled across her thoughts, and she turned toward the sound, unaware, as of yet, what precisely was being said. She perceived her elder daughter, face pinched and worried, but still filled with smiles. And now she was certain it was Christmas Eve, because Christine was dressed for Vigil Mass in a sweater of champagne gold.

"Mumzie, I made you some crackers with honey," Christine announced coaxingly.

"Take the spoon away." Her husband's voice, Jerry's voice, commanded from somewhere behind her, concerned and far more aware than anyone of her ebbing appetite.

"She'll want to lick the spoon," Christine responded,

with childlike certainty in the irresistibility and healing powers of the sticky sweet nectar. Passing the utensil to her mother, she watched with trusting brown eyes as the spoon was licked clean.

And somehow, despite the fact that almost everything had tasted like cardboard since she had fallen ill, the honey did taste good.

"See," Christine said to her father as she reclaimed the spoon. "I knew she'd want to lick the spoon."

How could she have resisted that hopeful face?

The honey-coated crackers consumed, somehow, she once more fell back onto the bed in search of sleep. But, the question came back to haunt her: if she slept, who would prepare for Christmas? She was sure that, without her, they could find a big Scotch pine to decorate for the living room. But what would go under it? She had not yet even wrapped their presents. There were so many things she had not yet done. Every year she would go out into the woods, behind their home, and cut evergreen branches—Scotch pine, white pine, and holly—with which to decorate the house. She would set up little snow villages—stored up in the attic for the rest of the year—on bookshelves, mantelpiece and small tables. She would shop for the largest turkey she could find, with the least amount of added who-knows-what in it. She would spend hours and hours in the kitchen, baking German cookies and Italian Christmas bread. What would happen to Christmas while she lay ill? She had to get up and prepare. But it was all she could do to remain conscious; after a moment, even that took too much energy—and she fell into troubled dreams.

She awoke to the gentle tinkle of Christmas music wafting up the stairs, like the tantalizing scent of freshly baked bread. She had slept through the night, for the first time since she'd fallen ill. And she had done nothing to prepare for Christmas. Salty tears pooled in the corners of her eyes. She had informed her children months before that this Christmas they would not receive so many gifts as usual. The economy was down and times were growing hard; they had to save money. Christine had informed her mother that all she wanted for Christmas were cookies and pannetone. Even that simple request had been impossible to fulfill.

In the midst of her sorrow, the door to her bedroom flew open and in poured her husband and three children. Matthias, her only son, picked her up in his strong arms and carried her down the stairs to a cozy nest of blankets on the living room sofa. She looked around in wonder. The Christmas tree sparkled in the corner, a good foot shorter than their usual eight-foot tree, but no less lovely. On the table beside her was a wax snow village, complete with its little Christmas train bearing tiny wrapped packages. On the desk nearby and the floor beside her were large poinsettias, brought home from work by Matthias, she imagined. She could smell brown sugar and candied cherries from the direction of the kitchen. It seemed Tess, her baby, had been attempting to recreate her mother's Christmas cookies. She turned back to the tree and noticed her packages, somehow wrapped, under the evergreen boughs. She glanced at Jerry, who smiled and winked.

"I'm sorry . . ." she began haltingly, not sure which apology to make first.

"We have the five most important things for Christmas," Christine interrupted. "The rest doesn't matter."

"We're together," Jerry added softly, and she felt her smile mirror his.

"Can I get you anything, Mumzie?" Christine asked, expectantly.

She smiled, basking in the warmth of her family, "What I'd really like is some toast with honey."

24, Décembre 2004
Age 22

Thé de Noël—Christmas Tea

Michel . . . The word was a ghostly whisper, a silent summons from the past wafting into his ears, like the warm tendrils of steam from a freshly brewed cup of tea. For a moment his eyes slipped into the past and his lips moved in barely audible mumbles, as if to answer; then the pale brown eyes refocused once more on the evergreen tree, lit softly in many-colored light.

Twining up through the branches of the sweetly smelling Douglas fir were strings of plump lights in a multitude of brilliant colors. It was his children who had struggled to twine the lights about the prickly branches, as they had done for the past several Christmases. So many Christmases past, he had relinquished the responsibility of weaving the lights through the branches of a Douglas fir, to begin its transformation from forest evergreen to Christmas tree. His eyes slid once more out of focus as he recalled another Christmas, even further in the past, when his father had relinquished the responsibility of the plump lights to him. Tiny white lights were said to be the most elegant of Christmas lights, but the fat colored lights held the magic of illuminating three generations of Christmases in his family, beginning with his father—his father, who was in heaven this Christmas. And though it had been many years since he had spent Christmas Day with his father, he felt an acute ache at his absence—at this, his first Christmas without a call from Dad.

The living room around him was divided into five haphazard piles of unwrapped presents, the discarded wrapping paper carefully folded into paper bags (at his wife's demand—he might have let the paper sit in festive crumples). Despite the hours of unwrapping that had already passed—presents were always opened one at a time, randomly alternating among the five members of the family—the tree still sheltered several brightly wrapped gifts, yet unopened. Wiffy—an affectionate name applied to her shortly after their wedding—who did the gift shopping for them both, had finished their Christmas shopping early that year. The beautifully wrapped packages had lain in piles in the dining room for what seemed like a good couple of weeks before Christmas Day, tantalizing everyone with anticipation. He recalled, with fond amusement, how his father had shopped for Christmas gifts: three o'clock in the afternoon on Christmas Eve, Dad would go out to the shops (shops that would close around five-thirty or six o'clock) and do all of his Christmas shopping. Anyone else would have been completely daunted by the overwhelming task, but not Dad.

It was that placid, lethargic time in the bustle of Christmas Day, somewhere between the second round of opening presents and the long anticipated (especially by him) turkey dinner. The stuffed turkey was cooking away happily in the oven and nearly the entire family had curled up, in various locations about the house, for a holiday siesta.

Wiffy had curled up in her love's comfy, white chair with a book that had since slipped from her limp fingers onto her lap. He placed a tissue in the book, as a marker, and tucked her soft, blue fleece robe up around her shoulders to protect her from the winter chill in the air. Asleep, she snuggled further under the fuzzy blueness, lost in peaceful dreams.

He made his rounds through the house in his usual slow, deliberate steps, stopping at each child's room to see that they were sleeping soundly. And if he found that they were curled up with their knees to their chests, like the tiny unborn babies they once were, he covered them with another blanket until their forms relaxed—just as he had done, it seemed, at least once per night since they were born. They were nearly adults now, but they would always be his children.

All were asleep; only he remained wakeful.

Having assured himself of the comfort of each of his dearest, he adjourned to the kitchen with the vague thought of tea and cookies. Wiffy made so many wonderful cookies for the holiday season, at least five varieties, and each more yummy than the last. Dad had loved those cookies. He remembered taking him some in the nursing home the previous Christmas. How Dad had gobbled them up, hungry in a way that no one can ever be for hospital food. He smiled at the warm memory. But Dad's personal favorite was probably Mom's brownies (the ones without nuts in them—Dad had never much liked nuts).

Michel . . . He was almost certain he heard, perhaps only within his own mind, the familiar name. A son named for his father—he was rarely called by his first name and instead answered to his middle name, so that father and son would not be confused. Most called him Mike, but his father had often preferred the French alternative—*Michel.*

"Dad . . ." he began in response, but whatever words might have followed caught in his throat.

He filled the teapot with water from the big kitchen

sink, set it on the stove to boil and began sifting through canisters filled with various types of tea, wondering for which he was in the mood. Earl Grey was arguably his favorite tea, and his father-in-law always bought him a box of Twinings Earl Grey tea every year for Christmas.

He crept quietly (as possible on the old hardwood floors) back to the living room in search of his Christmas present. With his left hand he found the small box of Twinings, as his right found a burgundy tin the size of his fist (perhaps slightly larger). He lifted the tin and examined it, shaking the contents and being rewarded with pleasant clatter from within. Ah yes, he recalled, a gift from his eldest daughter: a tin of loose Earl Grey tea. She had found it in a little bookstore called Webster's, nestled downtown from Penn State, where she attended university. Somehow it seemed the perfect Christmas treat to enjoy while he outwaited his family's rest period.

From within the kitchen a small, piercing whistle began that, he feared, would rise and wake the entire house. He rushed (none too silently) back to the kitchen to rescue the boiling water from the flame that irritated it. Having shifted the teapot to a cooler position on the stove, he dug through the drawers until he came up with a strainer. It came back to him as if it had not been so many years. He placed a pinch of the big leafed—not the finely ground tea that came in teabags, but big chunks of brownish leaf—tea into the strainer and poured the boiling water over it into his favorite mug. The heated water turned a shade of dark amber as it passed through the tea leaves. He dropped two lumps of sugar into the steaming liquid and felt the deep scent rise to his nostrils; he could almost taste it as he inhaled. . . .

Time fell away and he was in another kitchen, long

ago. He was the age of his children, on the verge of adult-hood, but not quite free of the wonder of childhood. It was Sunday morning breakfast. He was home from college for winter break, and Dad was making tea: scooping out a generous spoonful of loose Twinings Earl Grey—an option that, in a few decades, probably would no longer ex-ist—into a strainer for him and his son. They didn't speak, both preferring silent amity, as they ate their breakfast and traded sections of the Sunday paper. Dad sat hunched behind his paper, peeking over it every once in a while for a slice of toast, a sip of tea, or a glance at his son. They sat to-gether at the breakfast table, munching on toast and eggs and sipping the mugs of tea. Somehow those larger chunks of leaf made all the difference, or perhaps it was just that Dad had made the hot drink for him. But he could not re-call ever having a cozier cup of tea.

The tea had cooled to the point where it still seemed scalding hot, but would not actually burn his mouth as he drank it. He closed his eyes, as he sipped the tea, and saw his father at Sunday breakfast. *Michel* . . . He did not open his eyes, but took another sip—as if the taste could summon the past into the present and make it real. *I love you, Michel.*

His cup was almost empty of the dark amber liquid, but he did not notice. Without opening his eyes, he smiled. "Merry Christmas, Dad."

For John M. McVoy (1913–2002): eater of his wife's brown-ies (without nuts in them); drinker of tea (both loose and in bags); beloved husband, father, and grandfather.

December 24, 2005
Age 23

Merry Christmas, Angel

He could still hear the siren of the ambulance ringing in his ears as he bent over the small, limp form of a little boy. His fingers applied pressure to a relatively shallow cut in the boy's forehead. The cut may have been shallow, but it bled profusely—stains on the boy's shirt and hair attested that he had already lost quite a bit of blood.

Behind Jamie, his partner, Davis, was questioning the boy's mother: "How had the accident happened and when exactly? Did the child have any allergies?"

The woman stumbled through her answers, her eyes never leaving Jamie's fingers pressing almost painfully against her son's forehead.

The boy's eyelids fluttered and his head shifted, as if he felt an annoying insect preening itself a few inches above his nose. But Jamie's fingers did not release their pressure against the child's forehead. With his right hand he reached for some gauze tape.

The child's lips moved, but no sound came. He watched this strange man wrap his head in gauze wordlessly, wincing at the pressure applied.

Davis had finished questioning the mother and she knelt beside him as he worked, holding tight to her son's hand, as if the boy would slip away into darkness if she relinquished her grip.

"Will he . . ." she began in a trembling voice.

Understanding the almost-asked question, Jamie smiled and winked at the little boy, "Don't worry, we'll have him patched up and back home in no time. Santa will understand if he's out a little late tonight."

The door to the office slammed and Jamie's eyes flew open, brushing the cobwebs of dreams from his eyes.

Davis grinned at him from the door, a platter of cookies in one hand and two Styrofoam cups of hot chocolate in the other. "'Twas the night before Christmas, when all through the house not a creature was stirring, not even a . . . Jamie."

"That doesn't even rhyme," Jamie commented, as he accepted one of the cups of hot chocolate from his partner.

"Modern poetry, my friend, doesn't have to rhyme," Davis informed as he bit into one of the cookies he'd brought. "What were you dreaming about?"

Jamie smiled vaguely. "Visions of sugar plums."

Davis laughed as he swiped another cookie off the platter.

Jamie picked up a cookie himself and studied it. It was basically a chocolate chip cookie made with red and green M&Ms, nothing like the gourmet cookies his mother made. He could almost taste the rum icing on his favorite cookie. But when he bit into the circle in his hand it tasted of chocolate chips, not rum. He felt a stab of homesickness, even though home was not so very far away. It felt far when he was stuck at work—*you volunteered for this*, he reminded himself, *so that everyone else, except you and Davis, could spend Christmas Eve with their families—for half the night*. He looked at his watch: 22:00 hours. They would be watching Alistair Sim's *A Christmas Carol* right now, munching on cheese and crackers and sliced pepperoni. His two sisters would be taking turns wrapping presents at the kitchen table, sus-piciously watching the heads turned away toward the television to see if anyone was trying to peek. His mother would be falling asleep—possibly snoring gently, as she was getting over a cold. Late at night, she never seemed to be able to get through a movie without falling asleep at least once. Dad would be sitting on the rocking chair, with his youngest daughter's teddy bear on his lap (bears en-joyed watching TV as much as anyone), dressed in those red flannel pajamas that he saved only for Christmas. Jamie took another sip of his hot chocolate to hide his slight discontent.

They hadn't even had a call yet that night and he had been on duty for a good four hours. Not that he wished anyone ill luck on Christmas Eve, but he felt rather use-less sitting in the office sipping hot chocolate and eating store-bought Christmas cookies.

He closed his eyes again and felt his dream coming back to him—a little boy's bloodstained face and two piercing blue eyes watching his every move with fascina-tion.

Davis took a last sip of his chocolate and tossed the crumpled cup toward the waste bin across the room. Jamie raised an eyebrow in his friend's direction, as the bit of trash plunked against the rim and fell dejected to the hard floor. Davis began whistling "We Wish You a Merry Christmas," as he nonchalantly sidled past the waste bin, retrieved the fallen trash, and disposed of it properly. He suddenly stopped mid-verse, as he passed the littered desk where most of them sat to fill out their trip sheets. "Oh, I forgot," he apologized as he picked up a long, white envelope. "This came for you last week, when I was on duty with Parker."

Jamie slit open the envelope with his finger and a

picture card—the kind you could make at Wal-Mart with a photo on CD—fell out onto his lap, along with a folded piece of paper. The picture showed a woman with long, dark hair hugging a little boy, not more than three years old. The boy was grinning so much that the smile filled his piercing blue eyes. Across his forehead, Jamie could see the red line of a recently formed scar. The card said: *Merry Christmas from Robin and Jackie.* He smiled and unfolded the piece of paper, still looking at the child's irresistibly happy face on the card. In large letters—obviously traced over his mother's script—a message had been left in red and green crayon:

> Mommy says that angels are everywhere protecting little boys like me who get into big messes. I got home before Santa last Christmas, and he gave me a new sled with a strap to hold onto so I won't fall off and hit my head. I was a good boy this year, so I didn't see you. But I know that if I ever hit my head again, you'll be there to help me. And if it's Christmas, you'll make sure that Santa knows I may be a little late. Merry Christmas, Angel! Love, Jackie

Jamie smiled and folded the letter, as the memories of the previous Christmas Eve washed over him:

Davis was driving and Jamie sat in the back of the ambulance with the little boy and his mother. The boy's blue eyes stared fixedly into Jamie's own vivid, blue eyes. "Are you an Angel?" he asked quite seriously.

Jamie smiled tolerantly at the unusual question, and answered, "I'm an EMT."

A splutter of radio traffic startled Jamie out of his memories.

Davis was already standing and pulling on his jacket, brushing the last of the cookie crumbs from his lips. "They're playing our song."

Jamie nodded as he slid the letter into his jacket pocket. "Let's do it." Santa would understand if he was out a little late tonight.

For all angels and EMTs who are there to help us little, clumsy people out of our big messes.

December 21, 2006
Age 24

Knights of the Round Table

He drove home in the half-light before the rosy dawn of Christmas. It was so late, so early, that the sun had not yet begun to peek over the distant line of trees and only a dim light in the east suggested early morning. Pat's shift had ended at 0600 and he was driving home to Leslie and little Johnny. The boy was eight years old and barely ever saw his father, who worked the twelve-hour night shift—that little extra night differential pay would someday allow little Johnny to attend a good college and make something important of himself.

It had been a long night of citations for drunken driving and disorderly conduct. He had grown weary of the dirty looks he received for tickets and arrests—all in the name of public safety and protection. Some child might be alive tonight because he'd made that DUI arrest. But that hadn't stopped the offender's wife from giving him a scathing glance and a reprimand, "You should be ashamed of yourself: arresting a man for having a good time on Christmas Eve!" Anger had boiled under his carefully neutral expression, until he could feel his jaw ache with unspoken retorts.

After fifteen years on the force, the ingratitude of the people he had sworn to protect still left a bitter taste in his mouth, as it had left a bitter taste in his father's mouth—which the old man had attempted to wash away with vast quantities of Irish whiskey. Officer Patrick McLearen Sr. had worked homicide back when the city was not quite so civilized, when a jaunt through the wrong alley resulted in an absence of one's valuable possessions and sometimes one's life. The old man had been worn down by the inhumanity of the crimes he had dealt with day to day, until a good officer became a bitter man who drank too much and sometimes exercised his anger with a closed fist.

Patrick Sr. had rarely been around when Pat was a child, but he could recall one very special Christmas when he was very young and the old man had drunk nothing but his mother's hot spiced cider. He had woken up Christmas morning to find his father home—so rare in those days, when the old man was always willing to work an extra shift, for a few extra dollars, to help send his boy to college someday.

Under the tree had been a castle made of wood, painted over to look like stone. It had boasted crenellated battlements, for knights to stand guard and fair ladies to wave their favors, as their lovers set out on adventures. Inside the castle had been an armory filled with small swords, lances, battleaxes and maces exquisitely shaped from metal into miniature weapons. There had been a grand hall with thrones washed in gold, for a king and queen to sit upon. Behind the thrones had been a small tapestry with a red dragon rampant against a field of blue. There had been a council hall in the center of the castle, a rounded room with a round table at its center. The table had been carved from wood and engraved in Latin with four words around its edge: *muneris, tutela, fidelitas, veneratio.* These, his father had explained, were the cornerstones of a knight's life: *Muneris,* service to his king and country, and the woman he loved; *Tutela,* protection of those unable to protect themselves; *Fidelitas,* loyalty to the values believed in his society; and *Veneratio,* honor to himself, and to his family. One by one, Patrick Sr. had pulled tiny, carved figures, painted in brilliant colors, from his pockets. He had introduced each to his son by name, with a story of that knight's grand exploits. They had played with the castle all morning, with their other presents lying untouched, and temporarily forgotten, under the tree.

A smile eased the strain on Pat's face as he recalled that special Christmas. Looking back now, he wondered how many nights his seemingly crude and angry father had stayed up late, after returning from a long shift, painstakingly carving and painting those tiny figures. How many nights had he strained his eyes, in the dim light, reading Geoffrey of Monmouth, Sir Thomas Mallory, Chrètien de Troyes, Marie de France and other authors who had penned the legend of King Arthur and his knights? How many times, over and over, had he read those stories until—he had so committed them to memory—he could regale a small child with fantastic tales of noble knights and great deeds of valor?

Pat pulled into his driveway, still lost in happy memories of that Christmas and the days of play that had followed. He was careful to remove his shoes as he entered the house—careful so as not to wake his wife and little boy. His fingers found the little green extension cord, which he plugged into the nearby outlet. The Christmas tree, in the corner of the living room, awoke from the shadows—awash in red, blue, green and gold. Tiptoeing up the stairs, he could hear Johnny barely stirring—captivated by pleasant dreams. Passing his own bedroom, he slipped up rickety stairs to the chilly attic. Somewhere in this treasure trove of memories was his father's castle.

There were not so many boxes large enough to fit the miniature palace. In less than fifteen minutes, he was headed back down the stairs with a large, dusty box in his arms—a box large enough for a child to sit inside and play at racing cars or driving an ambulance.

Johnny was standing at the bottom of the stairs, rubbing the cobwebs of dreams from his eyes and staring expectantly up at the sound of descending footsteps.

"Did you see him, Dad?" Johnny asked in a whisper so loud, Pat was quite certain he could hear Leslie waking from the sound a room away.

"Him?" he asked, juggling the large, awkward box so as to view his son who barely came up to his waistline in height.

"Santa," he clarified with excitement. "I heard him on the roof, thumping around and looking for the chimney, but we don't have a chimney. So, I figured he probably came in the attic window." Pat raised his left eyebrow. They both knew the attic window was barely the size for a small sparrow to enter, much less a fat man in a red suit. "It's bigger than some chimneys and he can fit in those." Johnny defended his theory. "You must have heard him too—otherwise what were you doing up there?"

Pat smiled. "Well, Santa needed a little help with this present."

"What is it?" Johnny asked, excited by the size and the strange clinking coming with each of his father's long strides.

"Let's go down to the tree and we'll find out," he enticed with a twinkle in his eye.

"You don't have to go to bed?" Johnny asked, with even more excitement than he had shown for Santa.

"Not today," Pat answered. "Christmas isn't a day for sleeping."

75

They went down the stairs and Pat wiped the layer of dust off the large box and cut the old, brittle tape away. Johnny watched with such excitement that it made Pat wistful of another little boy, a long time ago in another living room, a little boy who lived in awe of his father's stories—a little boy who wanted to grow up to be a knight of the round table. Out came the castle, the armory, the thrones and the tapestry. Out came the knights, who he introduced by name: Arthur, Gawain, Lancelot, Galahad, Gareth, Agravain, Geraint, Kay, Tristan, and Bedivere. From somewhere in memory, he could hear his father's voice; he could hear the stories, too long forgotten, told in his father's slow, precise speech. Out came the table, lovingly carved in words his father had learned to give a bit of magic to his son: *muneris, tutela, fidelitas, veneratio.*

He traced the words with his finger. "This is the code of the knights of the round table," he told his son. His finger paused on the first word: *"Muneris,* service to king and country, and the women they love." He drew his finger around the edge and continued: *"Tutela,* protection of those unable to protect themselves; *Fidelitas,* loyalty to the values they believe; and *Veneratio,* honor to themselves, and to their families."

He slid his finger full circle again, reciting the Latin reverently. "The words are circular," he explained. "Each is a part, an extension of the others, as each knight is only a part of the council." Johnny picked up the little table in his hands and traced the words with his fingers, as if the texture could translate the meaning. As Pat began to tell the stories he was told so long ago, Johnny crawled into his father's lap and traced his fingers over the shield on Pat's uniform.

Pat recalled the daring exploits of the knights of the round table until the sun had climbed high into the sky.

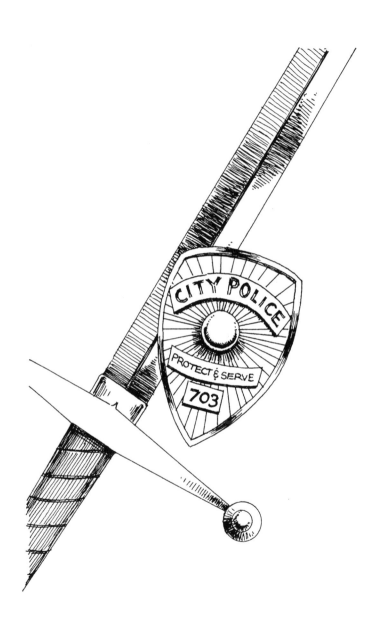

As the sun passed midday, and began to once again creep back to the horizon, Pat, happy, but beyond exhausted, settled into his old comfy chair in front of the tree and drifted into dreams of childhood. When he awoke late in the evening, he found a folded piece of paper on his chest. He unfolded the paper to behold a drawing in colored pencil of a knight, resplendent in silver armor, holding aloft a silver sword. On the knight's arm hung a shield that was a child's copy of Pat's police badge.

He could hear his father's voice, as if it were years ago, as if he were there: *"Muneris, tutela, fidelitas, veneratio."*

Although they may no longer wear silver armor, ride a white horse or carry a silver sword, knights still ride among us, serving and protecting, as in the days of Arthur. This story is for them, and for all who believe in Camelot.

December 23, 2007
Age 25

Where They Need No Star to Guide

As they offered gifts most rare
At that manger rude and bare,
So may we with holy joy,
Pure, and free from sin's alloy,
All our costliest treasures bring,
Christ to Thee our heavenly King.

Lucy trudged through the snow to Christmas Mass, her elegant black dress pants tucked firmly into a sensible pair of snow boots. She clutched a wreath of holly in her left hand and raised her face to the biting cold of the wind—it smelled of fresh cut spruce and pine, with a faint trace of gingerbread.

It was only a four-block walk to the church. She and Jeff had looked favorably on the possibility of walking to Mass each Sunday, rather than driving, when they had chosen a house in the village. Jeff especially was a firm believer in exercise as part of one's weekly routine, rather than an activity at the local YMCA. Jeff was not one to attend Mass every week; he was more apt to take a long walk by the lake, which was only fifteen minutes in the opposite direction of the church, and mutter his grievances or thanksgiving to the rippling water.

Jeff's lanky frame did not keep step beside her. It had been three months, and they had barely spoken or touched. Jeff worked such late hours each night in his father's shop that he fell into bed beside her, deep in exhausted sleep before she became aware of his presence. He had always risen earlier than she, leaving the house in the pre-dawn light, so that he could walk the longer path to the village, which wound by the lake. He would pause for a few moments on the old bridge and whisper to the water. He did it with such familiar reverence, that she had once contemplated if the heavens parted within the glassy reflection to give him glimpses of the realm beyond the veil.

In time past, she had sometimes risen with him and followed him across the winding trail down to the placid water. But so much had changed and she was almost relieved at his absence. She had allowed numbness to creep into her heart and mind over the past several months. She knew that Jeff's laugh, or smile, or the deep sadness in his blue-violet eyes might melt that cold façade—and then she would feel again.

Her right hand hung limp at her side, gloveless as she had somehow lost one of the pair someone had given her the previous Christmas. She received at least a couple pairs of gloves every holiday because of her well-known habit of losing them. Raised in New England winters, she never left the house without a pair of gloves. But she was so fond of feeling the texture of objects directly against her fingertips, that she often removed a glove and never remembered to retrieve it. Chilly goose bumps ran up her arm, as if a tiny hand had—for a moment—rested within her half-curved fingers. She shivered and rubbed her almost numb fingers against her leg.

She walked past the warm, welcoming light of the church doors and passed behind the structure to the small graveyard that lay there. The only light came from a small tree the parish children had decorated in the center of the graveyard. It had become an odd Christmas tradition, which had begun when Lucy's parents were young, and remained unbroken. As children, Lucy and Jeff had also sneaked into the graveyard the night before Christmas Eve to bring the joy of the season to the honored dead. She found the tiny stone easily, bathed in Christmas light, nestled in the soft shade of a sapling fir. The feathery branches fluttered in the wind and seemed to embrace the white marble, as if to shield it from the cold. Absently, she removed the glove from her left hand and began to brush away the thin blanket of snow with her bare fingers.

The rings on her third finger flashed with fiery brilliance, as they captured the light from the graveyard Christmas tree. She glanced down and away, but the red gems seemed to dance in the corner of her vision. Her engagement band resembled a rose, just bloomed, with the stem wrapped about her slender finger, twinned with a shadow band: two rubies, set in gold, resembling rosebuds. It had taken Jeff nearly six months in his grandfather's shop to perfect the little bouquet for her finger.

Jeff's great-grandfather had moved to the village over a hundred years before and opened a small jeweler's shop. For the first few months he had mended chains and refitted rings. Within twelve years, there hadn't been a young couple in the village that didn't buy their wedding bands, and usually their engagement ring, from Stevenson's shop. And, every once in a while, someone had bought one of the masterpieces that great-grandpa made late in the evenings after the shop was closed.

Jeff was a fourth-generation goldsmith and had surpassed his great-grandfather in creative skill. But Jeff didn't design contemporary settings that could have been marketed to some of the big chain jewelry stores. Often months in the making, Jeff's original designs were works of art that he never considered selling.

Despite herself, Lucy thought of the love that had gone into every detail of the rings. It had taken Jeff many late nights at the shop to complete them. So fixated on proposing with the perfect ring, he had inadvertently distanced himself from her as he became completely focused on his project. When Jeff finally proposed, Lucy had almost been afraid he was going to end their relationship.

Tears slid past her sooty eyelashes and seemed to freeze on her cold cheeks. Poor Jeff, it hadn't been his fault.

She gently laid the holly wreath in front of the headstone. She had made it herself, before closing the flower shop that evening. No one else had wanted to work on Christmas Eve and perhaps Mr. Donovan realized that she needed to be busy, or she'd fall to pieces. He didn't argue when she'd offered to close. In September she had brought flowers, fresh every couple of days. In October she had made autumnal bouquets and, once the winter cold turned the leaves from gold to brown, she wove wreaths of various evergreens. For the funeral she had brought roses, red roses. They had smelled so beautiful.

Lucy traced the letters on the gravestone with her fingers, as if by touching the stone she could caress his cheek.

Daniel James Stevenson
May he rest in peace:
"Where they need no star to guide,
Where no clouds Thy glory hide."
Born and Died September 17, 1987

"Merry Christmas, Danny," she whispered, her voice breaking. She remembered the weight of that small body against her chest, exquisitely perfect with miniature fingers and toes, but no fingernails or eyelashes. But he was too small, eleven weeks early with an almost certainty of permanent brain damage, even if they had put him on machines. They had made their terrible choice, she and Jeff. They had laid their tiny, perfect son on his mother's chest, with his father's arms cradling them both, and told him how much they loved him, as he tried to take his first—his last—breath.

They had buried him in a tiny casket, wrapped in a soft fleece blanket that would have covered him in his crib, with the teddy bear Jeff had purchased for him a week after he was conceived. And then they fell apart, as they both struggled to find a means to grieve.

Now it was Christmas Eve, and they were almost strangers.

Lucy slid into the back of the church as they began the second reading. She apologized mentally for being late; she hadn't realized how long she must have knelt in the graveyard. The readings and carols seemed to slide over her, without reaching her ears, as she gazed up at the picturesque Nativity scene that spilled over the steps to the altar.

God so loved the world that He gave us His only Son. That sacrifice now seemed terrible in its magnitude. To love this world so much that He would send His Son to be born and to die for it.

Only when faced with an impossible choice had she given her son to God. If they had hooked him up to life support machines, would she sit there now with a healthy baby in her arms and her husband beside her?

But Jeff, dear Jeff, she had not lost him so completely. Her son was in heaven, but her husband remained. So focused upon her lost child, she had hardened her heart against the man she loved most in this world. She looked around the church at the families in their holiday best: couples holding hands, children tugging at parents' sleeves and crawling under pews when they thought no one was looking. She looked again at the altar, at the three wise kings with their gifts, at the shepherd boy who had only his sheep to bring, and the animals who gathered just to look upon the newborn King. She gazed at Mary's face—the woman who had birthed a single child destined for a young death.

"We are all so busy at this time of year, shopping for that perfect gift for each of our loved ones. But what gift will we give to God on His birthday?" The priest's words rung across her thoughts like cathedral bells. "On the Epiphany, we celebrate the gifts of three wise men: gold, frankincense and myrrh. A children's story tells of a little angel, who gave a box of boyhood playthings to the newborn King. There is a song about a little drummer boy, whose only available gift for the infant Jesus was a song. A legend originated in the Renaissance about a traveling clown, who juggled before a statue of the Madonna and Child, on Christmas Eve, to allay the Child's sorrow. Each of these familiar stories tells not of gifts given from accumulated wealth, but gifts given from the spirit. The wise men gave gifts to the Child they knew to be the Messiah, which showed their reverence for His worldly monarchy, heavenly divinity, and the sacrifice He would make for all of our sins. The littlest angel gave a robin's egg, white stones and a pressed butterfly, which might have little value to any other child, but were his most treasured possessions. The drummer boy and the clown of God had no physical gift for the Christ Child. They had only their ability to entertain, to give a moment's joy with a song or a rainbow of juggled balls. That was the gift they brought to the feet of the King. What will each of you give to God, on this day? Christ said to His apostles, 'this is my commandment: that you love one another, as I have loved you.' This is the season of love. Every time we express love to one another, each time we forgive those who trespass against us, then we have given God the greatest gift we are capable of giving. So I charge you in this season of giving: give not only packages and cards, but give of yourself. Love your neighbors, as God loves you."

This was not a night of death, but of birth. As Christ rose from the dead on Easter morning, so too her son would sit at the foot of God's throne in heaven. She bowed her head. If souls could be trapped by thoughts, her little boy would never have reached the gates of heaven. She had haunted herself with the memory of her son, unwilling to forgive herself for the choice she had made, unwilling to find comfort in the arms of her husband.

She left the church and headed down the snowy path, past Christmas-lit houses, to the well-worn path that led down to the lake. There were no lights within her own house, as she rushed past it, and she knew where she would find Jeff, even at such a late hour.

He was standing on the bridge, not looking down into the star speckled blue-black depths, but staring down the path, as if he were waiting for her to appear. He had a package in his hand, a small fold of brown paper hastily wrapped.

She stopped a few feet away, almost shy to face him.

"I . . ." he stopped, perhaps shy himself and began again, nervously rubbing the little package between his fingers. "I'm sorry."

She blinked at him in complete incomprehension.

"I wanted to give you something to remember him, but it took so much longer than I expected—it always does," he dismissed the excuse before she could speak.

She shut her mouth, realizing that if she interrupted he might lose his nerve.

"I should have stayed with you. I should have held you and comforted you. I wanted to give you a memorial to him and I've almost lost you in the process. I—" his voice broke. "I'm sorry."

"I'm sorry, too . . ."

No longer shy, she grasped her husband in her arms and held him close. She felt his scent wrap around her, like a blanket, as she listened to his heartbeat through his heavy parka.

When they parted, he handed her the tiny package. She tore apart the paper awkwardly with her almost numb fingers—what had she done with her gloves?—and held a necklace up to the bright moonlight. It was a Nativity scene, wrought in white gold, with Mary and Joseph kneeling before an infant Jesus in the manger. The edges of the pendant curved up to form the roof of the stable, at its peak was a brilliant sapphire as the star of Bethlehem. She traced the lines of the pendant with her fingers, resting last upon the star. "It's perfect," she whispered.

Lucy turned to face the water and lifted her hair so Jeff could clasp the necklace around her throat. She felt the gentle weight of the pendant come to rest over her heart. The precious metal warmed instantly to her skin. She looked out over the water, so placid that she could see the heavens reflected in it. "Father," she whispered to the celestial depths, "into Thy hands I commend the soul of Thy servant, Danny."

Jeff wrapped his arms around her shoulders and held

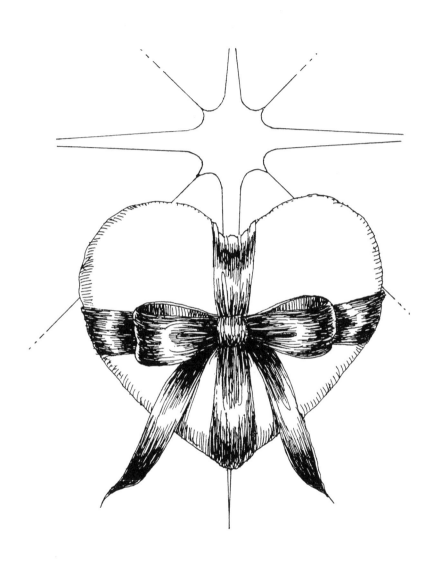

her close. His lips pressed against her hair and he stroked her tummy, as he had when she was expecting.

Somewhere across the water, they heard a child laugh for joy.

Holy Jesu, every day
Keep us in the narrow way;
And, when earthly things are past,
Bring our ransomed souls at last,
Where they need no star to guide,
Where no clouds Thy glory hide.

In the heavenly country bright,
Need they no created light;
Thou its Light, its Joy, its Crown,
Thou its Sun which goes not down:
There forever may we sing
Alleluyas to our King.

"As with Gladness Men of Old," William Chatterton Dix
(1837–1898)

December 24, 2008
Age 26

One Short Sleep Past

He stood before the door of his home, almost unwilling to enter and break the spell of perfection that lay without. New fallen snow, unbroken save for the prints of his own thick boots, lay over the entire landscape, like a quilt of white over a sleeping baby. The nearby trees hung heavy with snow; one was dying, its long, black branches bare of fine, green needles. He would make it a point to cut down that tree at the first thaw, when he and Andy would be able to dig out the roots from the now frozen earth. Its black branches hung heavy with snow reflecting the marmalade and rose of the sunset, giving it the illusion of flame.

He turned his back on the tree and faced the brilliance of the sun as it dipped below the mountains, leaving his home in elongating shadows. He took a deep breath, inhaling the rich fur scent of branches hung over doorways and windowsills—an ancient winter custom to ward off evil spirits. Even in this new country, the old ways followed them with superstition that was somehow comforting. He could smell the big loaves of Christmas bread that his mother-in-law, Bess, baked each year this night, and the deeper scent of beef and potatoes and various vegetables cooking in a large cauldron over the fire, as it did each Christmas Eve. Bess always made the big pot roast on Christmas Eve; for once it was piping over the fire, she was free to bake her special loaves. A soft melody drifted out of the house on the wafts of scent, an old Irish harp's delicate strings manipulated into familiar carols. He could see Jenny in his memory, with the old harp lovingly cradled in her lap like a child. The perfection of the moment belayed him at the door. He held the moment, taking in each flash of colored light reflected in iridescent snow, the mingling of each familiar and delicious scent and the soft strain of carols. It was as Christmas Eve had been for the past eleven years of his life and he was reluctant to enter his home and remember that it had changed.

But enter Danny did—removing his heavy boots at the door to avoid making puddles on the fine, wood floors that he and Old John had laid down together eleven years previous. He paused a moment, curling his toes within stockings, remembering those first days in this new and strange place. They'd been as new humans brought again to Eden—amazed and elated by a world untouched by man or war. God's country, Old John had called it, and all could see the resemblance.

They had come in the wake of the war between the North and the South, heading west in a covered wagon, like so many other families in those days: John, his wife Bess, and their three children. Jenny was the eldest, gentle in manner like her father, but clever in music—which her father claimed could only be attributed to a gift from the little folk, for he couldn't sing a note on key, much less pull one from a harp. Andy was the youngest, sometimes hot tempered, but with his father's gift with animals; like his father, he could calm a skittish beast with a touch and a muffled whisper. Then there was the middle child, Laura, and Danny, her Yankee husband. Also came Isaac, a freed slave from the plantation where Old John had worked outside of Winchester. John and Isaac had worked side-by-side, milking cows and delivering calves, for nearly half a century. Isaac was old now, as John must be old, though he had never thought of John as old. But Isaac still had a gentle touch with the expectant cows and, in so many years, he had become family.

Danny's own father had been a tinsmith in Gettysburg before the war. He had closed shop and fought against succession and against slavery. Danny could see his father now: tall and smart in his blue uniform, pistol at his side and rifle in hand. He had disapproved of his only son's choice to marry a Southern girl—still angry at the South for friends lost in the war. He could still see his father standing in the parlor with other gentlemen of Gettysburg, before the outbreak, smoking cigars and drinking port—as Danny had hidden under the staircase to listen to talk of war. His father had spoken loudly and firmly against slavery and for emancipation. But never had he seen his father clap a negro man on the back, or invite one to sit and dine with him and his family. Words meant so much.

But it was in the home of a Southern hired hand that the evident equality of the races was made clear; Isaac was as much a member of Old John's family as his flesh and blood. And when John had decided to leave Virginia and build a new life on a small ranch in the Midwest—that he lovingly christened the Silver Ranch—there was no question that Isaac would accompany.

Isaac was seated by the fire, reading slowly and deliberately from one of John's treasured volumes. The walls of the house were layered in bookshelves from floor to ceiling. Every time they went to town, Old John or Bess would carefully examine any books for sale to add to their collection. It was a beautiful collection of poetry, literature and histories. Before they had married, Bess had been a schoolmistress. She had taught all of their children, the hired hands, and even the children of neighboring ranches and farms for a penny each that went to the purchase of new volumes. Each evening, after supper, they would sit together before the fire, or sometimes in the heat of summer on the front porch lit with candles, and read aloud. Bess read plays, bringing a distinct voice and character to each part, from Henry V to Viola. Jenny would sing, her silvery voice accompanying the higher notes of the harp. And John would read poetry, his voice soft but clear, cherishing each word, each line.

On this night, as Bess baked her special bread and Jenny played carols softly on the harp, like lullabies, Old John should have been seated by the fire in his worn rocking chair, reading aloud to them all. His voice would rise and fall in a gentle cadence that made the house melt away into the fantasy of the stories he recited. John would always begin with the story of Christmas from the Bible, which somehow sounded like poetry when he read it, and then Clement C. Moore's *A Visit from St. Nicolas.* Then Laura might request E. T. A. Hoffmann's *The Nutcracker,* a fairytale type story of a doll who becomes a dream prince. Laura adored fairytales. And Andy, who loved the scarier tales, would ask for Charles Dickens' *A Christmas Carol.* Once Bess had the Christmas loaves in the oven, she would take over and read some of William Shakespeare's *Twelfth Night.* She would somehow space it out so that the entire reading of the play began on Christmas Eve and, with a few scenes read per night, ended on the Epiphany.

But tonight was different. Tonight Isaac sat in Old John's chair, painstakingly reading the Christmas stories; but without the lilt of John's voice, the stories seemed to lose some of their magic. Jenny's fingers moved over the harp, but her face was drawn with sadness and the harp seemed to reflect her mood in haunting, minor melodies. Andy sat in the corner, whittling away a piece of wood into no particular shape. His hands moved in small jerks, and his mouth was tight with not speaking. Laura stood in the kitchen, kneading dough into round loaves and occasionally adding water to the cauldron over the fire. She kept one ear toward the bedroom, where she had sent their two young sons to read quietly; from the sound, reading had evolved into a re-enactment of the battle of Agincourt. The boys never could sit still on Christmas Eve. They were the only ones in the house who seemed unmoved; but children viewed the world through different eyes.

Bess sat by her husband who lay abed, the frame pulled up close by the fire. She had covered John in quilts and the heavy Indian blanket, woven in the pattern of the sunset, for which they had traded a calf their first spring at the ranch. It was the warmest blanket in the house and still John shivered—chilled beyond the help of blankets and flame. Bess stroked her husband's forehead and held his hand. She spoke to him when he was wakeful and lucid, and listened attentively when he was not.

It was a week ago that the old Doc had made the long trip from town to see John, who had fallen so terribly ill so suddenly. The gravity of his face had told them John's fate before his words. He had been kind, but honest, and they had been grateful for that. And then had come the exhausting parade of mourners. For three days people had come: neighbors, seasonal hands, townsfolk, and Indians with whom they had traded over the years—friends all, bearing gifts of consolation and gratitude for knowing a man such as John. One by one they had come to say good-bye: whispering words of thanks, and clasping hands, proffering kisses on John's chilled brow. Bess had borne it all with dignity and grace, caring for her husband and being patient and sympathetic with the grief others felt.

Jenny had sat beside her mother, playing soothing music, ready to fetch another blanket or a cup of broth that John wouldn't eat. Laura had retreated to the kitchen, one hand baking and cooking Christmas dishes and refreshments for the friends who came to pay their respects, and the other keeping the boys out from underfoot. Isaac, entirely inconsolable, had taken up a position in John's old chair, lovingly stroking the books that John and Bess had taught him to read.

Danny and Andy had escaped to work. The Silver Ranch was Old John's dream, his paradise where they had begun a new life, away from hate and slavery and war. From a handful of cows, and a few acres of land, they had built John's dream; and Danny would not see that dream fail while John lived. It still felt like an escape: not to be in the house; not to see the sad, drawn faces; not to hear John's rasping breath; not to have to play host to a steady stream of mourners; to stand in the snow feeding the cows, or milking them, and forget for a few hours that everything was not as it had always been at the ranch.

John saw him standing undecidedly at the door, as if not aware of his welcome in his own house, and smiled. It was a slow, caring smile, as to make one feel loved and cherished. The Doc had given Bess morphine to administer to John for the pain. She must have just given him an opium pill, for the pain lines in John's face did not seem so pronounced. He smiled again and, for a moment, Danny could almost have believed that everything would be all right.

John called them all over to him: wife, daughters, son, son-in-law, grandsons and Isaac. His voice did not carry its usual volume, but they each heard and came to stand beside the bed, until he was surrounded by all those he loved best.

"We had good times, didn't we?" he asked of them rhetorically. "Good times." His voice seemed to strain, as if each word were an effort, as if the words themselves were steps up a steep, winding staircase. "Take care of each other . . . always. . . ."

"Are you afraid?" Little John asked softly; his mother placed a hand on his shoulder, and the other on his brother's.

"No," John whispered. "But you are . . ." His eyes took in his wife and all of his children. " 'One short sleep past, we wake eternally and death shall be no more . . .' " He gasped at the last word. Then he looked expectantly at his grandchildren.

And it was the younger, Joseph, who answered slowly, *"Death be Not Proud."*

"John Donne," added Laura softly, with tears in her dark eyes.

"Do not fear for me," the words came so softly that they could have imagined them. "I go to be with God. . . ." John's voice trailed off, as if he would have said more, then his eyes closed from the effort and he slid into dreams.

The boys stood there a moment, awkwardly uncertain, and then hurried off quietly to play. Laura leaned against Danny, her head nestled just under his chin; he could feel her eyelashes fluttering with tears.

In that moment, it seemed as if the Indian thunder gods were coming to take John into the Spirit World. The old, dead tree, unable to support the weight of so much snow, had fallen, frightening the cattle and causing them to stampede. Danny flew to the door and stared unbelieving at the impossibly fresh imprints in the snow.

"They . . ." He couldn't express himself. This night of all nights . . . Why hadn't he cut down that damn tree last year when it began to fail, or tied it back so that it couldn't fall suddenly and spook the herd? Insanity crept into his mind and he wondered if they could wait until morning to fetch the cows home. But the temperature was dropping and there would be wild animals, and thieves, who would make quick work of John's small herd. "I . . ." He felt suddenly lost and small, as if he had shrunk to the size of his own children.

It was John's voice that spoke, with that gentle volume that could reach every corner of the house. "Go, Danny Boy,"—he used the pet name the family called him after the favorite Irish ballad—"Bring the lasses home." John always affectionately referred to the cows as his lasses, as if they were blushing debutantes instead of dumb, four-footed creatures.

How could he leave? He looked at John, completely lost, but John smiled confidentially.

"Bring the lasses home. 'Do not send to know for whom the bell tolls . . .' "

" 'It tolls for thee.' " Danny finished with a half-smile. John Donne. "I'll bring them home," he promised. His brow furrowed. "If . . ." his voice trailed off unable to complete the sentence, unwilling to say such a thing aloud.

But John nodded, understanding. "I love you, Danny Boy."

Danny couldn't remember his father ever expressing himself so candidly. The comparison was unfair, and he knew it. They were different men from different worlds, though their country was the same. But he only wished that he could have shared feelings so freely with his own father.

"I'll be back in a few hours." He kissed Old John on the forehead—his skin was so cold. Danny paused. John smiled weakly back. It was infectious, despite the lack of strength in it, and Danny felt his own lips twist in response. "I love you, John."

Andy followed Danny into the night, an unspoken companionship between them. Blessedly, the snow had stopped falling while they had lingered within and the direction of the stampeding cows lay clear before their feet. Without a word, they saddled Oscar and Prairie Dawn and rode after the fleeing lasses.

The lasses had paused their hastened retreat at the edge of a steep canyon where, in the summertime, John would sometimes meet with the local Indians to trade. There were no Indians in the canyon now. Snowdrifts lay deep all around, masking the depth of rock shelves within layers of white. He counted the heads of cattle methodically, his mind far away with a man dying in his wife's arms by a roaring Christmas fire. He came up one calf short. He refocused his mind, forcing it away from that roaring fire, to the cold canyon. The tally was still one short.

He looked full at Andy and saw the same dismay growing on his lean face. The wind whipped through the canyon, wiping all chances of speech away with the hoof marks of the cows and horses. Danny gestured for Andy to lead the herd home and lowered himself down the canyon wall to find their stray calf. He could almost believe that he could hear the little creature crying under the whistle of the wind. And yes, there it lay half-buried in a snowdrift. He picked the little fellow up, cold but unharmed by the slight fall, praying just for a moment to possess some of John's magic with animals. Perhaps he did, for the creature lay still upon his shoulders, like a lady's shawl.

The trek home was slow. He led the horse—the calf slumbering, curled around his neck—unwilling to move the creature should it waken and realize that it was not John who held it thus.

Dawn was breaking, like fire raging against the sky behind him, as he came once more in sight of home. The other cattle were penned and already fed. As soon as he lifted the calf from his shoulders, the little thing awakened and cried out for its mother, who gave Danny a rather stern look—as if *he* had led the little fellow away in the night. Slightly disgusted at the stupidity of four-footed creatures, he surrendered the calf to its mother, unsaddled Oscar and rubbed him down.

He knew before he entered the quiet house; in truth, it felt as if he had known before he left in the night. Isaac sat unmoving in John's rocking chair. Andy and Jenny were huddled in the corner, silently rocking, arms entwined. Laura clutched at him—beyond speech, beyond tears. Bess smiled at him sadly, but gratefully. The bed no longer lay by the big fire, but back in the master bedchamber. He walked slowly into the room where John lay, as if asleep. He had come too late: too late to say good-bye one final time; too late to ever hear John's laugh, or see his smile, or listen to him read. How could he have been gone this night of all nights? But he had brought the herd home. And Old John had not died alone, or in vain, but surrounded by loved ones, and adored. He reached over and kissed John's cold forehead. "I did it, John," he whispered. "I brought your lasses home safely." John's dream would live on through his children, through Isaac, through Danny, and through his grandchildren.

The farm's work was calling: cows to be milked and, no doubt, manure to be raked up. They would be making butter and cheese soon, to sell at the Spring Fair in town. If there were a little left over after necessary purchases were made—and in recent years there was always just a little bit left over—they would add the extra coins to Bess' pennies from reading lessons and buy some new books. The boys were anxious for the latest Jules Verne adventure and Andy was slowly collecting all of the Edgar Allen Poe pocket books. There was a new Mark Twain novel, about a prince and a pauper who trade lives for a day, that Laura was dying to read. But the ranch—and the milking and preparing for the Spring Fair—could wait just a few more minutes.

Danny sat by the bedside table and picked up the book John had been reading last. He opened it to the marked page and began to read. His voice wavered, but grew steady. In the next room, he could hear the boys wakening and digging through their bulging stockings—stuffed to the brim with new socks, pocket books and candy sticks from town. Soft voices rose in song from the main room, accompanying the old, Irish harp. The scent of evergreen boughs and Christmas bread, lathered in fresh butter, wafted out of the kitchen. He continued reading steadily as the room and the scents and the sounds fell away, replaced with visions of the tale he recited.

The sun rose high on Christmas morning, flooding John's Silver Ranch with golden light.

For John Michael McVoy (1943–2008) called Michael, Mike, sometimes Michel and, most of all, Daddy: reader of poetry and stories to his children, whatever their age; lover of all four-footed creatures great and small; eater of pot roast and pannetone; namer of the backyard bunnies Oscar and Prairie Dawn; owner of the Silver Ranch, even though it was only a Playmobile toy; and, most of all, beloved friend, son, husband and father. Here is your first Christmas western. I love you, Daddy, and I miss you. Merry Christmas!